A VIEW TO KILL FOR. . . .

Inside, narrow, irregular stone steps wound upward in the dark. Frank's shoulders brushed the central pillar on one side and the rough tower wall on the other. Every so often, a tiny slit in the wall gave him a glimpse of the city or the sea far below.

The top platform was no more than six feet across and already crowded. Gail and Perry made their way to the edge, next to Delaplane, who was scanning the coastline with a pair of binoculars. Frank found himself hemmed in and saw with a touch of envy that Joe had managed to reach the knee-high parapet with its stunning views.

As more people arrived at the head of the stairs, the crowd shifted. All at once Frank heard an alarmed shout. He spun around and saw with horror that Joe was falling sideways and would be over the parapet in an instant. Frank's heart sank as he realized that he couldn't possibly reach his brother in time to save him. . . .

Books in THE HARDY BOYS CASEFILES™ Series

Available from ARCHWAY Paperbacks

THE HARDY BOYS CASEFILES NO. 94

A TASTE FOR TERROR

FRANKLIN W. DIXON

AN ARCHWAY PAPERBACK
Published by POCKET BOOKS
New York   London   Toronto   Sydney   Tokyo   Singapore

103225

AN ARCHWAY PAPERBACK *Original*

An Archway Paperback published by
POCKET BOOKS, a division of Simon & Schuster Inc.
1230 Avenue of the Americas, New York, NY 10020

Copyright © 1994 by Simon & Schuster Inc.
Produced by Mega-Books, Inc.

ISBN: 0-671-88205-8

First Archway Paperback printing December 1994

10 9 8 7 6 5 4 3 2 1

THE HARDY BOYS, AN ARCHWAY PAPERBACK and colophon are registered trademarks of Simon & Schuster Inc.

THE HARDY BOYS CASEFILES is a trademark of Simon & Schuster Inc.

Cover art by Brian Kotzky

Printed in the U.S.A.

IL 6+

A TASTE FOR TERROR

Chapter

1

FRANK HARDY took a croissant from a big basket of the delicious, flaky rolls and put it on his tray. His blond-haired brother, Joe, was already heading for the cash register in the cafeteria. They had arrived half an hour before at Paris's Orly Airport after an overnight flight from New York. Now they had about an hour to kill before the second leg of their trip to Tunisia.

Frank followed Joe to the register and paid for his croissant and coffee, then scanned the cafeteria and spotted Perry Housman, the former astronaut. Housman wasn't an easy man to miss. Like Frank and Joe, he topped six feet, and his years in the military had left him with posture that made him appear even taller. His thick, prematurely white hair contrasted sharply with the deep tan of this devoted outdoorsman.

Frank and Joe had met Housman when they were investigating a mysterious series of crimes at the U.S. Space Academy in Huntsville, Alabama. A few weeks after they'd returned to their hometown of Bayport, they had received a note from Housman. He was chairing the upcoming hundredth anniversary conference of the International Explorers Guild, which was to take place in Tunisia. Would they like to go?

"Would we!" Joe had exclaimed after reading the note. "I've heard about those meetings. Some of the world's most exciting people get together to talk about their latest expeditions."

"Not to mention that amazing banquet they have every year, with exotic dishes from all over the world," Frank had added. "And it's a chance for us to visit a new country."

Housman was now sitting with several other people at a large table near the windows. As Frank and Joe crossed to him, Frank saw that Housman's seventeen-year-old daughter, Gail, was with him. The Hardys had met her during the graduation ceremony that had taken place at the end of their stay at the U.S. Space Academy. She had long dark hair and midnight blue eyes, a combination Frank found very attractive. She noticed the Hardys, waved, and pointed to two vacant chairs at their table.

"Hey, everybody," she said when they reached

the table. "Meet super detectives Joe and Frank Hardy. Are you on the flight to Tunis, too?"

"It looks that way," Frank replied, sliding his tray onto the table and sitting down.

"Hi, fellows," Housman said in a gravelly baritone. "Glad you could make it. We're going to have a terrific conference this year. Do you know Sally Komatsu and Doug Rourk?"

Sally was tense looking with very short black hair. Doug had red hair, a sprinkling of freckles across a snub nose, and a cheerful grin.

Joe whistled as he dumped his backpack on the floor and took a seat. "Sally Komatsu, the diver—right?" he said. "I read an article in *Undersea* about your work on ocean-floor volcanoes. Are you going to be talking about it at the conference?"

"I am," Sally replied, stirring sugar into her cup of coffee. "I'd like to get other people as excited about it as I am."

"Sally has some remarkable projects in mind," Housman said. "It's just a matter of finding money to carry them out."

"That's always the problem, isn't it?" Doug remarked. "Usually, what gets funded is whatever looks hot to the guys who pass out the money. Meanwhile, lots of less showy but really worthy projects end up in a file drawer somewhere."

"Doug's a filmmaker," Gail explained to Joe and Frank, obviously admiring his abilities. "His documentary on an Egyptian immigrant community in New Jersey won several big prizes. Maybe you saw it on public television. It was very moving."

"Thanks, Gail. I'm glad you liked it," Doug said. "I owe it all to my uncle Patrick. He lent me his life savings to make that film. Hey, maybe Frank and Joe can 'detect' how I'm going to pay him back."

"That's not really our line of work," Frank said, laughing. "Are you working on a new film?"

"Let's say, I'm hoping to," Doug told him. "I'll start shooting as soon as Uncle Patrick wins the lottery. I wonder why he's taking so long?"

Everybody chuckled.

"Well, just in case your uncle Patrick doesn't come through, there's somebody who might take up the slack," Perry said. He waved to someone across the room and called out, "Thor—Thor Sonderstrom! Over here."

Frank put down the croissant he'd been munching on and glanced over his shoulder. The man who was moving toward them was of medium height with broad shoulders and a barrel chest. He was dressed in jeans and a blue blazer over a striped tennis shirt. From a distance, his blond hair and athletic stride made him look about thirty-five or forty. As he came closer, Frank noticed the deep wrinkles around his eyes and decided that he was much closer to sixty.

Sonderstrom shook hands with Perry, then nodded to the others as Perry introduced them.

"Thor is the head of the Leif Eriksson Foundation, which is a major source of support for our conference," Perry explained. "I think you'll get your money's worth from the conference, Thor."

"I'm sure we will," Sonderstrom replied with a faint Norwegian accent. "We are not so rich that we can afford to waste our assets on projects that aren't worthwhile."

Joe asked, "Can you always tell in advance which projects will be worthwhile?"

Sonderstrom studied Joe coolly for a moment. Then he said, "No, not always. But we make sure that someone who has disappointed us once never disappoints us again."

Frank thought that Sonderstrom sounded as if he'd watched too many bad movies about organized crime bosses. Across the table Gail gave a slight shiver. In reply, Frank rolled his eyes, then grinned.

After a short, uneasy silence, Perry said, "Well, Thor, you've certainly piled up quite a track record. You must be doing something right."

Sonderstrom gave a quick nod, then said, "Please excuse me. I must call my office before we leave."

As he walked away, Doug said, "Isn't Thor the name of the Norse god who always heaved thunderbolts at people?"

"Hush, he'll hear you," Gail said in an undertone, trying unsuccessfully to hide her grin.

"Thor Sonderstrom has probably done more to

help increase our knowledge of the world than anybody else in the last thirty years," Perry said in a clear, carrying voice. "I don't know of an important archeological or geographical expedition that the Eriksson Foundation didn't help."

Frank glanced around. Sonderstrom was standing at a phone booth a couple dozen feet away. He had his back to them, but Frank had the strong impression that he was listening. Had Perry deliberately made his remark loud enough for Sonderstrom to hear? If so, why? Was he trying to butter up the foundation head?

A few minutes later Sally checked her watch and said, "We'd better head over to the departures lounge. We don't want to miss the plane."

"I don't think they'll leave without us," Perry said with a tolerant chuckle. "Half the people on this flight are on their way to the conference. Still, it's bad manners to keep the pilot waiting," he added, pushing back his chair.

Just a few hours later the jet began its descent into the airport in Tunis, Tunisia's capital. Joe peered out at the sea and the long coastline. "I had no idea France and North Africa were so close," he said to Gail, who was sitting between him and Frank.

Gail raised her eyes from her guidebook. "Tunisia is in the northernmost part of Africa," she replied. "According to this, on a clear day, you can stand on the beach there and see all the way to Sicily."

"I'll have to try it," Joe said. "Does your book say anything about where we're going?"

"I haven't read that far yet," Gail admitted with a sheepish smile. "But Dad told me that we're going to be staying in what used to be the summer palace of the bey. Now it's been turned into a totally up-to-date conference center."

"The palace is on a bay?" Joe asked.

Gail grinned. "No, silly. The bey is what they called the kings of Tunisia in the old days."

"I don't think I've ever stayed in a palace," Frank said. "I hope it isn't habit forming. Oops, here we go," he added as the airplane swept low over a beach edged with palm trees.

Once they touched down, they passed quickly through customs and immigration. A chartered bus was waiting to take them and the other conferees to the bey's palace, about sixty miles south of Tunis. As they pulled away from the airport, a cheerful hum of conversation filled the bus.

Joe turned to Gail, who had taken a seat just across the aisle from him, and asked, "Does everybody at these meetings know everybody else?"

"Not quite," she said with a laugh. "But if you come to them often enough, you do get to know a lot of people. My dad's been bringing me since I was about eight. You see that gray-haired man two rows up? That's Sir Thomas Twining, the mountain climber. And the woman across from him is Suzanne Lavigourie, who holds the women's record for sailing the Atlantic solo."

"Pretty distinguished company," Joe said a little uneasily.

Gail seemed to sense his reaction. "Oh, don't worry," she said. "Most of them are really nice, even if they're famous."

The three of them kept chatting as the bus traveled south along the coast. Finally, though, it slowed to make a left turn. Joe glanced out the window. A long drive led between two rows of towering royal palms to a dazzling white building. On each of its three levels, intricately carved columns framed the many windows. Along the front of the building, a row of symmetrically trimmed bushes burst with brilliant red blossoms. As the bus circled a fountain and came to a stop next to a monumental flight of steps, Joe caught a glimpse of the radiant sea just beyond the palace.

Frank murmured, "The bey sure had an eye for real estate. I hope we can grab some beach time between conference sessions."

"Count on it," Joe replied with a grin.

The Hardys pointed out their luggage to one of the uniformed staff members, then followed the crowd up the steps. Inside, the huge entrance hall had high ceilings and marble walls. The floor was made of alternating squares of dark and light marble flecked with what looked like gold. At the far end of the hall, a row of arched doorways looked out onto an interior courtyard.

There, white stone walks wound between flower beds planted in precise geometric shapes to a splashing marble fountain in the center of the courtyard.

"I think I could get used to this," Gail said, glancing around. "What about you guys?"

Frank glanced up at the massive chandelier hanging high above the center of the room and quipped, "Not if it meant I had to change the lightbulbs."

A man in a cropped white waiters' jacket stopped next to them. His tray was loaded with small handleless cups. The three teens each took a cup, and Gail said, "This must be mint tea. My book says it's really delicious."

Joe took a sip. The hot beverage was so sweet that he had trouble tasting the mint. He was about to comment when he heard angry voices just behind him. Thor Sonderstrom was facing a guy of about thirty with thick black hair and a jutting chin. They were posed like a couple of boxers just before the bell.

"You're a fool, Fred," Sonderstrom said in a voice heavy with contempt. "Why advertise your own incompetence in front of everybody?"

"You're nothing but a two-bit tyrant," the other man replied. "Without the foundation's money behind you, nobody would give you the time of day. And it's about time somebody told you so."

Sonderstrom said something in what Joe guessed

was Norwegian, and it didn't sound complimentary. As the foundation head turned away, the other man remained rooted to his spot for a moment. Then he leapt forward, tackled Sonderstrom around the waist, and pulled him to the floor.

Chapter

2

As SONDERSTROM and his attacker struggled on the floor, the Hardys moved in quickly to break up the fight. Frank grabbed the younger man's coat collar with one hand and his arm with the other, then pulled him off Sonderstrom and to his feet. As he did so, Sonderstrom struggled to a standing position and lashed out with a hard punch to the pit of the guy's stomach. He gasped and bent double. Sonderstrom was about to follow up with another punch when Joe lunged in front of him and grabbed his wrist.

"Okay, take it easy," Joe said. "The fight's over."

Sonderstrom tried to jerk his hand away, but Joe's grip was too strong.

Frank tugged the younger man away, keeping

a tight hold on his arm just in case he tried to start up again.

The man glared at Frank. "What's the idea, holding me while that bozo slugs me?" he demanded. "Who are you anyway?"

"Just somebody who's trying to stop a fight," Frank said in his most reasonable voice. "Come on, let's take a walk to cool off."

As he started to turn the guy away from Sonderstrom, a man in a dark blue suit, with a round face and a receding hairline, hurried over.

"Fred, I'm surprised at you," he said, tapping him on the chest. "Shocked, in fact. I know that you and Thor have had some differences, but that doesn't excuse creating a scene."

"Do you mind, Bob? I'd rather discuss it another time," Fred replied.

"I think we'd better, for the sake of the guild's image. We have lots of media here, you know." The balding man frowned and walked away.

"Who was that?" Frank asked as he urged Fred toward an uncrowded corner, well away from Sonderstrom.

"You don't know?" Fred replied in surprise. "That's Robert Delaplane, the anthropologist. You must have heard of his book, *Passage in Time*. It won a Pulitzer Prize last year."

Frank thought for a moment. "Is that the book about the tribe in Central Asia that's been cut off from the rest of the world for centuries?"

"That's it," Fred told him. "Bob's the only

Westerner who's ever studied them. He's been very careful not to give away their exact location. Otherwise, some unscrupulous people might try to exploit them."

Frank wondered if writing a best-selling book about a tribe counted as exploitation, but he kept the thought to himself. "Why are you so mad at Sonderstrom?" he asked.

The man's face darkened. "Don't get me started."

"I'd say you owe me an explanation," Frank said smoothly. "After all, I just saved you from getting your face smashed in."

The man leaned against the wall, his shoulders suddenly rounding forward. At last he sighed and said, "My name's Fred Estival, and until two weeks ago I was executive secretary of the Leif Eriksson Foundation."

Joe came over in time to hear this. "The foundation that Sonderstrom heads?" he asked.

"That's right," Fred said tautly. "I put five years of hard work into that job, then got fired because I disagreed with one of Thor's decisions. Not that it was the first one I disagreed with," he went on. "Far from it. But this time it got me canned."

"What was the decision you disagreed with?" Joe asked curiously.

Fred gazed at Joe as if he were noticing him for the first time. "Hey, who are you guys anyway?" he demanded.

Frank and Joe introduced themselves and explained that they were guests of Perry Housman.

"The teen detectives?" Fred replied. "That's right, he told me you were coming. I'm glad I didn't get my hands around Thor's throat just now, or you might have had a homicide to investigate."

"What did you and Sonderstrom disagree about?" Frank prompted.

Fred shrugged and brushed his hair back from his forehead. "I can't tell you the details," he replied. "But Thor Sonderstrom is famous for making sudden decisions that wreck people's lives. In most granting agencies, if the executive committee votes to fund a project, that's that. Not at Eriksson. Thor's been known to cancel funding at the last minute—"

"What do you mean?" Joe asked sharply.

"Well, take what he did to Alfred Portago, the gorilla expert, last year," Fred replied. "Portago was already off in Africa when he got the news that Sonderstrom had changed his mind about the project. And to get his expedition off the ground, Portago had gone deep into debt. He expected to pay back what he'd borrowed when the grant money came through. He was so upset by Sonderstrom's decision that he quit his university position and dropped out of sight altogether."

"That's terrible," Joe exclaimed. "Couldn't anybody do anything?"

"I tried," Fred told him. "And got nowhere. Once Thor makes up his mind, it's like arguing with a block of concrete."

"So," Frank said after a pause, "what are you doing at the guild's anniversary conference?"

Fred seemed to be taken aback but then shrugged and replied, "I came to find a new job, but I won't if I don't start mingling. See you later."

Before they could react, Fred turned and walked away.

"How about that?" Joe said, shaking his head.

"Maybe we should keep an eye on him," Frank commented. "He may be planning to take another poke at Sonderstrom."

"Probably not right away," Joe replied. "Sonderstrom's pretty well protected at the moment."

Frank noticed the foundation head at the center of a little group that included Robert Delaplane, Sally Komatsu, and Doug Rourk. Sonderstrom made some remark, and all the people around him laughed. To Frank's ear, their laughter sounded incredibly phony.

"You fellows are lucky," Perry remarked, moving over to stand beside them. He raised his chin to indicate the group around Sonderstrom. "Unlike them, you can sit back and enjoy the conference. You don't have to spend every

15

minute worrying about what you say and to whom and how it might affect your chances of getting money to carry out your work."

"I think I'd hate that a lot," Joe replied.

"Me, too." The former astronaut chuckled softly and added, "Though I'm just about in the same boat myself. I sent Thor a proposal a few weeks ago for an educational project on space exploration. I'd really like the chance to carry it out. Some of the foundation board members told me they like it, but I have a hunch it's a little too tame for Thor. He tends to go for projects with a lot of glamour—ancient lost temples, running uncharted South American rivers, expeditions in the Himalayas, stuff like that."

"You're not hanging on him," Frank pointed out.

"Nope. Call it pride," Perry replied with a grin. "Or maybe I'm trying to use reverse psychology on him. You know—make him come to me and beg me to take the foundation's money. That'll be the day!"

Gail appeared in the doorway and spotted her dad with the Hardys and came over to join them.

"Hey, guess what?" she said. "I just met this neat kid named Ahmed. His family's worked in this palace for generations, and he knows everything there is to know about the place. He said he'd take us on a short tour. Isn't that nifty? What do you say?"

"I say, let's do it," Joe replied.

"You kids go ahead," Perry said. "There are a few wrinkles about press coverage for the conference I still need to iron out."

Frank and Joe waited while Gail tried to recruit a few more people for the tour. Sally and Doug both agreed, as did a young guy with shaggy blond hair and a deep tan.

"Guys, this is Hans Esslinger, from Austria," Gail said to Joe and Frank. "He spends his time climbing mountains, then skiing down them with a camcorder strapped to his shoulder."

"That sounds really exciting," Joe remarked. "Will we get a chance to see any of your footage at the conference?"

"Oh, yes," the young Austrian replied. "But I hope you will be tolerant. I am not a real film-maker, like Doug. I am only a ski bum who likes to show people some of the interesting places he's been."

Doug laughed and clapped Hans on the shoulder. "Places like the high Andes, you mean!" He turned to Frank and Joe and added, "Wait till you see some of the things this guy's done. They're enough to make an eagle scared of heights!"

"We shouldn't keep Ahmed waiting," Gail pointed out when the laughter died down. She led the little group through an arched doorway into a long corridor. The boy who came to meet them was about twelve, with dark eyes and hair and a gleaming smile. He was wearing heelless sandals, loose white pants, and a Chicago Bears T-shirt.

"Welcome, friends, to the palace of the former bey," Ahmed said.

"You speak English very well," Frank told him.

The boy's smile widened. "Thank you, sir," he said. "I study the English since the age of eight. I speak French as well and, of course, Arabic, the two principal languages in our country. Next year I intend to begin the Japanese. When I am big, I hope to be the minister of tourism for Tunisia."

"You've already got a lock on the job," Doug joked. When Ahmed stared at him blankly, he explained, "I mean you've got a good shot at it."

"Oh, I see," Ahmed replied. "I hope so. Now to begin. You have just come from the first reception room. We go now to the state dining room, where you will dine tonight."

As he started down the corridor, he looked over at Frank, who was right beside him. "Please, you are from where?"

When Frank told him he was an American, Ahmed continued, "If you have letters during your stay, will you save the stamps for me? I 'collectionate' stamps from many countries."

"Sure," Frank agreed. "But it would be better English to say, 'I *collect* stamps.' "

Ahmed nodded. "Oh? Thank you, I will note that." He stopped next to a pair of tall, intricately carved wooden doors and raised his voice. "This is the state dining room. It is kept locked, because the tapestries on the walls are antiques beyond price."

"How do you know so much about the palace?" Hans asked him.

"I was born here," Ahmed explained. "My grandfather served the last bey, and my father helped make this a conference center."

Ahmed produced a key and opened the doors. Frank followed the others inside. The room was almost as big as a basketball court. The tables were already set with gold-rimmed china, gleaming silverware, and sparkling crystal. Name cards in little porcelain holders marked each place.

"Please notice the ceiling," Ahmed said. Obediently, everyone looked up. "It is of wood, carved by the finest craftsmen of the time, then covered with many hundreds of leaves of gold. It is told that every worker was washed before he left each day to save any flecks of gold that were on his skin."

Sally aimed her pocket camera at the ceiling and snapped a picture, then set it down on the table and began to stroll around the room, glancing at the name cards as she wandered. Finally, she returned to the group.

"Next, we see the throne room," Ahmed announced, leading them out the door.

Sally, the last to leave, stopped in the doorway

and said, "Oops, I forgot my camera. Go on ahead, I'll catch up."

"Please be sure the door locks when you leave," Ahmed told her. "The tapestries are very valuable."

The throne room was even more elaborate than the state dining room. The walls were covered with brightly colored mosaics laid in intricate patterns. Tall arched windows offered a view of formal gardens with white gravel paths that stretched down to the sea. Frank was a little disappointed to see that the room was filled with rows of folding chairs and that there was no throne on the platform beneath the windows. In its place was the latest in audiovisual equipment.

"You explorers will meet here," Ahmed said proudly. "Nowhere in my country is a more modern conference center. Now we go to look at the courtyard and its fountain from the Roman days. Then you will want to rest before dinner."

The room Frank and Joe had been assigned was furnished like any modern hotel room. Only the high ceiling, with a lazily turning fan in the center, and the tall windows with louvered shutters suggested they were in a palace. They unpacked their bags, then took turns in the shower.

As they finished dressing, a gong sounded downstairs. They found their way back to the state dining room. A man in a white dinner jacket met them at the door, checked their names on his list, and directed Frank to table 7 and Joe to table 4.

The large, ornate room was already more than half full. The light from hundreds of candles reflected off the carved gold ceiling and sparkled on china, crystal, and silver. Over the buzz of conversation, Joe heard a flute playing an exotic melody. He located his table and started toward it. Thor Sonderstrom was already sitting there, as were Sally Komatsu and Hans Esslinger.

Joe was pulling out his chair when he noticed Sonderstrom suddenly stiffen. Trying not to appear obvious, he kept his eyes on the man.

The foundation head had been unfolding his napkin when he crushed it angrily—but not before Joe saw the crude image of a grinning skull drawn on it in blood red.

Chapter

3

JOE FROZE for a second, then sat down as if he had seen nothing unusual. His thoughts raced. Who could have drawn that skull on Sonderstrom's napkin and why? He examined Sonderstrom's face, which was set in an expression of angry determination.

All through dinner Joe noticed that the foundation head was studying everyone at the table with barely concealed suspicion. He seemed to be focusing especially on Sally. Did he have some reason to think she was the one who had drawn the grinning skull on his napkin?

In addition to Sally, Hans, and Sonderstrom, Joe's tablemates were an elderly Canadian who had explored the Arctic on dogsled and an Australian woman who was a champion balloonist.

Neither of them seemed to know Sonderstrom well or to be very concerned about impressing him.

Sally, on the other hand, appeared as tense as a fiddle string. She picked at her food and, whenever she could, spoke to Sonderstrom about her underwater exploits.

"On one trip last year, a couple of hundred miles northeast of Oahu," she said at one point, "my deep-sea craft got totally stuck in gooey volcanic mud two thousand feet down."

"Wow! What did you do?" Joe demanded.

She barely glanced at him, then returned her gaze to Sonderstrom. "I was sure I was a goner," she continued. "Then I figured out a way to dump my ballast, a ton and a half of lead pellets. With that gone, the craft had more than enough positive buoyancy to pull free of the mud, but the ride back to the surface was pretty wild."

Sonderstrom said, "Most interesting, Ms. Komatsu." Then he deliberately turned away from her and said to Hans, "Do you always climb the mountains you intend to ski down? I should have thought a helicopter ascent would be faster and easier."

As Hans began to answer, Joe kept his eye on Sally. She turned red and shot Sonderstrom a brief flash of anger. Then she noticed that Joe was watching, and her expression smoothed over. A few moments later she was chatting casually with the balloonist about diving off Australia's Great Barrier Reef.

Between dessert—a flaky pastry stuffed with a mixture of chopped nuts and honey—and coffee, Joe excused himself and went over to Frank's table. Frank noticed him coming and met him halfway.

"Anything wrong?" Frank asked in a low voice.

"Maybe," Joe replied. He quickly told Frank about the skull on Sonderstrom's napkin. "It might have been a joke," he concluded. "But even if it was, it's not very funny. Especially after the way Estival picked a fight with Sonderstrom."

"You think it was meant as a real threat?" Frank asked.

"I think we'd better assume it was until we find out otherwise," Joe replied. "Should we tell somebody about it?"

Frank hesitated. "That can wait until we know more. But something is definitely going on here, and I'd like to find out what."

At that moment Ahmed, wearing a white jacket that buttoned up to the neck, walked by with a tray of small coffee cups balanced on one hand. He gave Frank and Joe a proud smile and said, "Tonight is the first time I am passing the coffee for guests."

Joe grinned back. "Way to go, guy," he said.

As the boy walked away, holding himself straight and tall, Frank said to Joe, "Why don't you go back to your table and keep a close eye

on Sonderstrom and the others? I'll corner
Ahmed when he's free and see what I can learn
about the security arrangements in this room."

"Check," Joe replied. He returned to his seat
just as Sally was explaining to Hans that the study
of underwater volcanoes was vital because of
their connection to earthquakes and tsunamis.

"I thought that tsunami was a Japanese deli-
cacy made from raw fish," Hans said.

"That's sashimi," Sally said impatiently as the
others at the table chuckled. "A tsunami is what
people used to call a tidal wave before we discovered it has nothing to do with tides."

As Sally continued her explanation, Joe glanced
around the table and decided that the others were
starting to think of Sally as a braggart and a bore.
Didn't she see the damage she was doing to her-
self with the very people she was so desperate
to impress?

There was a break at the end of dinner while a
television crew from Germany taped an interview
with Perry and some of the conference speakers.
Joe and Frank found a quiet place to talk.

"Well," Frank began, "I know how much you
hate locked-room mysteries, but we just may be
facing one. According to Ahmed, the state dining
room is kept locked at all times."

"Not at *all* times," Joe pointed out. "Ahmed
unlocked it himself when he gave us that tour.
And the doors were open when people came
down to dinner this evening."

Frank nodded. "Right. So it seems as if Sonderstrom's napkin had to have been fiddled with on one of those occasions."

"Frank," Joe said, "remember when we were on that tour—Sally went around the room, checking out the name cards? Then, when we left, she said she had to go back for her camera. She was in there alone long enough to draw that skull on Sonderstrom's napkin."

"I know," Frank replied. "And it would have been easy enough for her to have left her camera on purpose. I wondered about that at the time. So she had the opportunity. What I don't get is this—what on earth is her motive? Why would she want to threaten Sonderstrom when she's trying to get money from his foundation?"

"Do we know that she is?" Joe asked. "It looked like it at dinner tonight, but I'd like to be sure."

"Let's ask Perry as soon as he's free," Frank suggested.

The former astronaut was just finishing his interview. "I have to admit," he said, "standing up in front of a group of people as distinguished as the members of the Explorers Guild is a lot more scary than piloting the space shuttle. For one thing, you don't have a team of a few hundred experts backing you up!"

The listeners laughed sympathetically. The bright lights went out and the sound engineer retrieved the tie-clip mike from Perry's jacket.

Perry stood up, shook hands with the interviewer, and said, "I know you'll enjoy the conference. I always do."

Perry turned to leave, then noticed Joe and Frank. "Well, fellows, how are you enjoying the conference so far?" he asked.

"It's great," Joe replied for both of them. "And we're really looking forward to the talks. Is Sally Komatsu on the program?"

"Why, yes, she's on a panel about unexplored frontiers," Perry replied. "I hope she can relax a little. She's really been on edge about getting funding for her plan to study undersea volcanoes. The word is that Thor Sonderstrom is leaning toward a yes, but with him, you never know. A lot of people will give a sigh of relief if he changes his mind and turns her down."

"Why?" Frank asked. "Do they dislike Sally that much?"

Perry was shocked. "Not a bit! She's a very devoted diver and fun when she relaxes. But if the Eriksson Foundation sinks a hunk of its budget into her project, there's that much less for everyone else. Sad, but there it is. Hey, we'd better hustle," he added, glancing at his watch. "We don't want to miss the first presentation—especially since I'm introducing the speaker!"

The Hardys joined the rest of the group in the throne room to find seats. The evening's speaker was Dr. Sylvia Monfort, a tall, slim woman. She was part of a team that had pioneered using computer-enhanced satellite photos to find the traces of vanished civilizations. Frank and Joe listened and watched intently as she described how they had located an ancient city buried in the jungle of Central America; a Roman settlement beneath the green fields of England; and even the route taken by the great cattle drives from western Texas to Dodge City, Kansas.

As the applause swelled at the end of the presentation, Joe said to Frank, "I wouldn't mind having an enhanced satellite picture of Bayport. There are supposed to be a bunch of sunken ships from colonial times in the harbor. I bet some of them would show up."

"Treasure hunting?" Frank asked with a laugh.

"Nope, just curious," Joe replied.

They stood up and hung back from the crowd that was flowing toward a long table of cold drinks and pastries at the back of the room.

"That reminds me," Joe continued in an undertone. "I've been thinking about that skull on Sonderstrom's napkin. What if Sally put it there with the idea that Sonderstrom would blame one of the people who's competing with her for funding? That would explain her motive."

Frank tugged at his earlobe for a moment, then said, "If that was her idea, she didn't do a very good job, did she? I mean, there wasn't anything about the skull that pointed to a particular culprit. In fact, from what you told me about the way he eyed her, Sonderstrom may have suspected Sally."

"That's true," Joe said. "But what if we've got it backward? Maybe someone else did it, trying to frame Sally."

Frank rubbed his chin. "Or how's this for a scenario? Whoever did it was one of the first to go in when the doors were opened for dinner. He filched a napkin from one of the tables, went off somewhere private to draw the skull, then came back and substituted that napkin for the one at Sonderstrom's place."

"But that means it could have been anyone," Joe said.

"Anyone who's angling for money from the Eriksson Foundation," Frank replied with a wry smile. "But from what we've heard, that means half the people at this conference!"

Early the next morning Frank and Joe changed into bathing suits and went down to the beach. Out over the sea, the sun was already well above the horizon, and the air was warming up. The two brothers raced each other down to the surf, dived in, and swam out about fifty yards. The water was chilly, so they body-surfed back to shore.

As they were toweling off, Joe said, "You'd better pinch me. I think I'm dreaming."

Frank looked around. Coming along the beach toward them was a smiling man in jeans, a T-shirt, and a checked Arab headdress. He was leading two camels, one dark brown and one light tan.

"Hello," he called as he drew nearer. "You want to ride? Very gentle camels, much fun and not expensive."

"Maybe later," Joe replied.

"I will be here," the man told him. "Also my friends Brigitte and Gina, named for famous movie stars."

Laughing, Frank and Joe returned to their room and dressed for breakfast. Back downstairs, they found that tables had been set up on a shaded terrace facing the sea. They got in line behind Robert Delaplane and filled their plates with strawberries, slices of melon, and fresh pastries. Gail, a few places ahead of them, waved and pointed to a table near the edge of the terrace. Frank nodded in agreement.

As Frank was pouring himself a cup of coffee, he noticed Thor Sonderstrom come out onto the terrace. Sonderstrom was hard to miss. He was wearing a white linen suit and a wide-brimmed panama hat with a multicolored madras band. Under his arm, he carried a slim leather portfolio. He paused at an empty table near the one Gail had pointed to and put his hat and portfolio down, then started toward the buffet.

Frank stiffened as he saw Fred Estival start toward Sonderstrom. Were Frank and Joe going to have to break up another fight? At the last moment Delaplane intercepted Estival and took him aside. Perry, who had apparently seen the whole incident, went over to Sonderstrom and started a conversation.

Frank glanced around the terrace. Sally, Doug, and Hans were a few places behind him in the line. Doug and Hans were busy choosing their breakfast, but Sally was watching Sonderstrom and Perry with an oddly intense expression. Frank had the impression that she wanted to join their conversation but didn't dare.

"Hey, guy, you're holding up the line," Joe said, nudging Frank with his elbow.

"Sorry," Frank replied. He added cream and sugar to his coffee, then he and Joe carried their trays over to the table where Gail was waiting.

Frank was finishing his melon and wondering if he should go back for another slice when he heard a shout followed by the crash of breaking dishes. He spun around, then gasped and leapt to his feet.

Thor Sonderstrom was standing rigidly next to his table, his hat in his left hand. On the table, black against the white cloth, was the deadly form of a scorpion, its poison-tipped tail arched, ready to strike.

Chapter

4

JOE AND FRANK sprang up and sprinted toward Sonderstrom's table. But before they got there, the foundation head made a sweep with his hat. The scorpion tumbled off the table and tried to scuttle to safety. Sonderstrom instantly raised his foot and crushed the insect with his heel. Then, red faced, he gazed around the gathering circle of startled spectators.

"Who is responsible for this?" he demanded. He took in Fred Estival and glared. "You, Fred? You're certainly childish enough to think of something like this."

"Go jump in a lake," Fred replied through clenched teeth. "With any luck, you'll run into a hungry crocodile. Though any self-respecting croc would think twice about eating you."

Robert Delaplane, in cream-colored slacks and a colorful Hawaiian shirt, stepped forward. "Now, now, Thor," he said jovially, taking his arm. "I'm sure there's some reasonable explanation. Scorpions are often found in climates like this."

Sonderstrom gave Delaplane a look that made him take a step backward. "In the desert, yes," he said. "But on a breakfast table? Under my hat? Don't be more of a fool than you have to be, Robert."

He started to stalk off into the palace. In the doorway he paused and looked back. "I'm not going to sit still for this. And when I find out which of you is responsible, I'll see to it that you regret your stupid behavior for a very long time."

"Thor, wait!" Delaplane called. As a hum of conversation rose on the terrace, Delaplane scurried after Sonderstrom.

"Some temper," Joe said as he and Frank returned to their table and picked up the chairs they had overturned in their hurry to help Sonderstrom.

"Ugh!" Gail said, shivering. "I hate scorpions. They give me the creeps."

"Me, too," Joe replied. "Once I found one in my salad. It was weeks before I'd go near a bowl of lettuce."

"I didn't know they were so common around here," Gail continued, glancing nervously at the ground near her chair. "I'm going to have to start

33

shaking out my shoes every morning before I put them on, just in case."

Frank took a sip of coffee, then said casually, "Sonderstrom didn't seem to think the scorpion got there on its own. He seemed pretty sure that someone put it there."

Gail was startled. "That's ridiculous," she said. "Who'd do a thing like that?"

"Easy," Joe told her. "Somebody who's mad at him. And from what I hear, that includes quite a few people. But how did our joker manage to put the scorpion under Sonderstrom's hat? That table's in plain sight."

"That might not be so hard," Frank replied. "Look how near the table is to the entrance. Everybody had to walk by it. What if you simply paused next to it with your back to the crowd? Chances are no one would pay any attention. And even if somebody did notice, he wouldn't be able to see what you were doing."

Joe frowned. "It could have happened that way. But in that case, whoever did it must have come down to breakfast this morning with the scorpion."

"I still think it could have crawled there by itself," Gail said. She gave a nervous glance up at the palms that edged the terrace and added, "Maybe it fell from a tree."

Frank grinned and patted her hand. "I don't think scorpions climb trees," he said. "And I doubt if a three-inch-long scorpion could wriggle its way under that hat. Its tail would get caught on the brim. Too bad my back was to Sonderstrom's table, or I might have noticed something. What about you, Gail? Your seat's facing the right way. Did you see anyone?"

She gave him a nervous smile. "Me? No, I'm sorry, Frank. I didn't see a thing. I was busy trying to decide whether I really wanted breakfast. I think the answer's no."

She pushed her chair back and stood up. "I must still have a little jet lag," she added. "I think I'll go rest before the morning session. See you later."

Joe watched Gail as she crossed the terrace and entered the palace. Then he turned to Frank.

"Gail couldn't have put that scorpion there," Joe said. "I saw her carry her tray straight from the buffet to the table, and she didn't get up after that. But she's sure acting odd. There wasn't anything wrong with her appetite before."

Frank nodded. "I know. But maybe seeing a scorpion upset her. Or maybe the jet lag really did just hit her." He picked up a piece of pastry and added, "We'd better do some eating ourselves. This could be the start of a long, eventful day."

After breakfast Frank and Joe circulated, talking to people about the morning's incident. They met at the door to the throne room just before the morning session was to start.

"Any luck?" Frank asked.

Joe gave a discouraged shrug. "Everybody wanted to talk about Sonderstrom and the scorpion," he reported. "But no one saw anything. To tell you the truth, I got the feeling most of them were rooting for the guy who put it there."

"Same here," Frank replied. "I even talked to one of the staff, but he didn't know anything. There were no waiters on duty because breakfast was a buffet." He stepped aside to let a little knot of people enter the throne room. "We ought to talk to Perry about this and offer our help. He's in charge of the conference, after all. With all these media people looking on, Perry's bound to be concerned if someone's out to make trouble."

"Right," Joe said. "But maybe we're going about this all wrong. I mean, how did the culprit manage to get hold of a live scorpion? I doubt if he trapped it in the garden or ordered it from room service."

Frank nodded. "Good point, Joe. Do you suppose somebody in the nearest town sells scorpions?"

"As pets, you mean?" Joe replied with a look of disbelief.

Frank gave an exasperated sigh. "*I* don't know—maybe fishermen use them for bait. But if there is someone who sells them, I doubt if he sold more than one yesterday to a foreigner. After the session, maybe we can check out the market in the old part of town—what's it called? The *souk?*"

Joe glanced through the open doors and said,

"Yeah, great idea. But right now, we'd better find seats. They're about to start."

That morning's speaker was an Italian diver, Commander Giovanni Fortiche. He had recently discovered a cavern on Italy's Mediterranean coast that could be entered only through a long, perilous underwater passage. On its walls were perfectly preserved prehistoric paintings. The audience gasped at the slides of beautifully drawn mammoths, bisons, and cave bears.

When the floor was opened to questions, Sonderstrom was the first on his feet. "This is most impressive, Commander," he said in a tone that rang with sarcasm. "But it leaves me wondering about the authenticity of these paintings. Did you find any evidence of another entrance to this cavern, one that is now sealed? Or are you asking us to believe that these prehistoric artists had access to scuba gear?"

There was a murmur of disapproval as Sonderstrom sat down. But Fortiche's expression and tone of voice didn't change.

"Neither, Mr. Sonderstrom," he said. "But at the time we are discussing, much of Europe—*all* of your part of Europe, I'm afraid—was covered with a thick layer of glacial ice. As a result, the level of the Mediterranean was about sixty feet lower than it is today. So you see, prehistoric men could have entered the cavern without the help of modern diving equipment. They would not even have needed to get their feet wet."

Like a lot of others in the room, Frank laughed and turned to observe Sonderstrom's reaction. He wasn't laughing. He sat with arms folded, his face impassive. But Frank sensed that he was making a mental list of the laughers and that in the future they would not find it easy to get a grant from the Leif Eriksson Foundation.

When the session ended, Frank and Joe searched for Perry but couldn't find him. So they left the palace grounds and walked on a wide, dusty boulevard a quarter of a mile to the center of the nearest town. They stopped at a small tourist office to get a map, then entered the *souk* through one of the gates in the high stone wall that surrounded it. Frank had the feeling that they had time-traveled a few centuries into the past. Narrow, irregular lanes led off in every direction, met, divided, or dead-ended in courtyards. In places, the low stone buildings touched overhead to form arches that shaded the pavement from the fierce sunlight. On the street level, every building seemed to house a shop of some kind.

A man with a bushy moustache stepped out of one of the shops and took Joe's arm.

"Welcome," he said with a toothy smile. *"Bienvenu. Wilkommen.* Here you find best prices on rugs, brass, everything fine. Only come look."

"No, thanks," Frank started to say.

Joe stepped in. "Wait—we're trying to find a scorpion. Do you know where we should look?"

After a moment of confusion, the man's smile returned. "Yes, of course! Inside, please."

Joe gave Frank a triumphant look, then they followed the man into the tiny shop. The shelves that lined the walls were filled with pottery, brass vases, and jewelry. Colorful Oriental rugs hung from the ceiling. Frank circled a large straw basket of embroidered leather slippers and stopped next to a glass display case. The shopkeeper unlocked it and reached in, then produced a silver pin in the form of a scorpion.

"Guaranteed sterling," he said proudly. "Very artistic. I have also all other astrological signs to bring good luck."

"Great," Joe said. "But we're looking for a *real* scorpion. One that's alive."

"Alive?" the man repeated. "Oh, no, sir. No good. They are poison. Anyone who sees one kills it. But in genuine sterling silver to take home to a special friend?"

He held up the pin again and tried to put it in Joe's hand. While Joe tried to fend him off, Frank wandered over to a set of shelves next to the open doorway and casually examined the colorful pitchers, ashtrays, and incense burners.

A flash of red caught his eye. He stepped into the doorway and looked. A girl in a crimson blouse and long black skirt had just passed, almost running. Something about her seemed familiar. As Frank watched, she tripped on one of the uneven cobblestones and almost fell. Recovering her balance, she glanced around. It was Gail. Her face was pale and set in an anxious expression.

Frank took an involuntary step forward, but Gail was already hurrying up the lane.

"Joe?" Frank called over his shoulder. "I just saw Gail, and I think she may be in some kind of trouble. I'm going after her."

"Coming," Joe said quickly. The shopkeeper, still holding up the scorpion pin, tried to get in front of Joe, but Joe sidestepped him and followed Frank into the street.

"That's her turning left into that alley," Frank said. "Come on!"

By the time they reached the mouth of the alley, Gail was at the far end. She was standing with a tall, slim guy dressed in white. Frank couldn't see his face, but something about him seemed familiar, too.

The guy put his arm around Gail's shoulders and led her through an arched doorway.

"Should we follow?" Joe asked.

"I think so," Frank replied.

But when the Hardys reached the doorway, they found that it led into a dilapidated courtyard. The windows of the buildings around it were bricked up, and there was no one in sight. Gail and her companion had vanished.

Chapter

5

"WHERE DID THEY GO?" Joe demanded, scanning the deserted courtyard.

"Well, they didn't sprout wings and fly away," Frank replied. "There must be another way out." He began to circle the courtyard, trying each of the doors. The first three were nailed shut, but the fourth swung open easily. Behind it was a dark, narrow hallway. To the left, a steep staircase was blocked off by a barricade of rough boards.

Frank found his keyring and switched on a tiny but powerful penlight. "Let's give it a try," he said over his shoulder.

With Joe close behind him, Frank walked to the end of the hall and found that it turned left. A few feet farther on, it opened onto another courtyard. This one was not much bigger than a

Ping-Pong table and had what looked like a hastily boarded-up well in the center. Frank and Joe carefully circled the well and tugged at the door on the opposite side. It screeched open, revealing a short flight of stone steps that led up to a narrow alley open to the sky.

"Do you have any idea where we are?" Joe asked as they started along the alley.

"Nope," Frank replied. "But judging by the map, the whole *souk* isn't much bigger than half a dozen square blocks American-style. No matter how lost we get, we can't be that far from the outside."

A few steps farther on, the alley joined a wider street lined with shops. Frank stared in both directions. "I don't see Gail," he reported.

"I don't either," Joe replied. "I hope she's okay. Do you think that guy she met knew we were keeping an eye on her and deliberately gave us the slip? I can't think why else they'd take such a weird, roundabout route."

Frank thought for a moment. "We were pretty far behind her," he finally said. "I doubt if either of them spotted us. But I agree that they were trying to lose anybody who might be following them. And now we know one important fact about the guy Gail met. He sure knows his way around the *souk!*"

The Hardys spent the next half hour wandering through the alleys of the *souk,* searching for Gail and asking shopkeepers about a place that sold live scorpions. They batted zero on both counts.

The exploration wasn't a total waste of time, though. Along the way Joe bought a sharp brass letter opener inlaid with colored stones to give to their father, Fenton Hardy. At another shop, Frank couldn't resist a T-shirt with two camels, a palm tree, and the words *Souvenir of Tunisia* in English, French, and Arabic.

"You're going to wear that?" Joe demanded, not believing what he saw. "It looks more like a tent than a T-shirt."

Frank grinned and said, "This would never fit me, but Chet's birthday is coming up. Do you think it's big enough?"

At the main entrance to the *souk,* Frank paused to look around. "Let's go sit at that café across the road," he suggested. "It's got a good view of the gate. If Gail is still inside the *souk,* we've got a chance to spot her leaving."

They took a table on the sidewalk and ordered two lemonades, then sat back to watch the passing crowd. Many of the people were dressed in Western clothes, but Frank noticed quite a few women wearing loose, long, dark-colored robes. The big shawls tied around their heads left only their faces and hands exposed. One woman, dressed in a robe, was with two schoolgirls in T-shirts, jeans, and sneakers. Frank wished he could take a picture of the little group, but he suspected it would not be considered polite.

"There's Gail," Joe said suddenly. "She's alone."

Her red blouse made her easy to spot. She paused at the edge of the road to let an exhaust-spewing taxi go past, then started across. As she came closer, she noticed the Hardys, waved, and smiled. Frank found himself hoping that the smile was for him.

"Hey, you guys," she said, coming over to their table. "Look what I just bought."

She showed them a large scarf in shades of blue, turquoise, and green. "Isn't it gorgeous?" she asked. "The weaver's loom was in the back of his shop. I watched him working."

"That's a lot more impressive than this T-shirt I just bought for a friend back home," Frank said with a laugh. He unfolded it and showed it to her, then added, "I think I saw you in the weaver's shop a little while ago. Wasn't somebody else with you?"

Gail blinked and turned away. "With me? No, I was by myself. You must have made a mistake. I'd better run. I have to take care of some letters for Daddy. He'll be worried about me."

As she hurried away, Joe turned to Frank and said, "Very subtle."

Frank defended his tactics. "Look, now we know for sure that she wants to hide the fact that she met that guy."

"That doesn't mean the two of them have anything to do with harassing Sonderstrom. Maybe he's just someone from the conference her dad doesn't approve of," Joe suggested. He glanced at his watch and added, "We'd better get back. By now, somebody's probably slipped a crocodile into Sonderstrom's bathtub."

Frank nodded. "Let's go. "

As the Hardys entered the palace, they saw Perry crossing the hall. They called to him, and the former astronaut waited for them.

"What's up, fellows?" he asked.

"You were there this morning when Mr. Sonderstrom found that scorpion under his hat, weren't you?" Frank began.

Perry said, "I certainly was. It's amazing the places those things get into."

"We're not so sure it got there on its own," Joe replied. "It wasn't the first thing that happened to Sonderstrom either." He told Perry about the skull on Sonderstrom's napkin.

"Now hold it," Perry said. "I know Thor suggested that somebody who has it in for him put the scorpion there. But I think he was overreacting, and so are you. Who'd do such a thing?"

"What about Fred Estival?" Frank asked. "He doesn't make any secret of the fact that he's furious at Sonderstrom."

"Furious enough to throw a punch, yes," Perry replied. "But Fred's not the sort to do anything underhanded. I know you're very talented detectives, but you can take a break from it now."

"We'd be glad to," Frank told him. "But not if it means shutting our eyes to what's going on."

"Nothing's going on, take it from me," Perry said emphatically. "This conference is going to be a big success. We've got journalists from all over the world here covering it. The last thing we need is a scandal to take attention away from the serious work of the guild."

"We know how to work quietly," Joe said.

Perry took a deep breath. "I'm sure you do, and I know you want to be helpful. But in my opinion, the best thing you can do is forget the whole thing. By the way, you haven't seen Gail, have you?"

"Sure, just a few minutes ago," Joe replied. "She was on her way back from shopping."

"Oh. Well, that's all right. Thanks."

As Perry walked away, Joe said to Frank, "So much for Gail's story of hurrying back to keep her dad from worrying. She simply wanted to get away from us and our questions."

After lunch Joe and Frank joined the other participants in the throne room. The afternoon presentation was by a couple who had spent a year traveling around Eastern Europe with a band of Gypsies. After it was over, Frank and Joe worked the room, quizzing more people about the scorpion incident. Their luck was no better than it had been that morning.

"Nobody saw a thing," Joe complained when he and Frank got together again. "In fact, they seem to have forgotten the incident ever happened. All they wanted to talk about is the big banquet tonight. Is there really going to be baked lizard, or was somebody pulling my leg?"

Frank laughed. "I don't know, but it doesn't sound any weirder than some of the other dishes I heard about. The banquet is really the main event here. Some of the guild members have been out in the kitchen all day working on their special dishes. They must be driving the regular kitchen staff crazy."

"We ought to talk to Ahmed again," Joe suggested. "Maybe he knows something more than the staff member you questioned this morning. He may have even heard some interesting tidbits from the other waiters."

"Good idea," Frank replied.

The Hardys started toward the service wing of the palace and found the dark-eyed boy just outside the big swinging door that led to the kitchen.

"Tonight is a very grand occasion," he told them proudly. "A reporter from New York asked me questions today. She was beautiful, and she talked very fast. And two more television crews are here now from Paris and Tokyo. Do you think I will have my picture shown all over the world?"

"Could be, Ahmed," Joe replied, patting his shoulder. "It couldn't happen to a nicer guy."

Ahmed grinned and feinted a punch at Joe's arm.

When Frank asked him if he'd heard anything from the waiters, Ahmed said that he'd been off duty since he'd served the coffee the night before. "The whole serving staff is resting to prepare themselves for the great banquet," he said, grinning. "Now I must do the same."

With that, he took off down the corridor.

Frank shrugged and said, "Let's go change into our swimsuits. Maybe we'll find some better witnesses at the beach. And if not, at least we can get in a swim."

Ten minutes later, as the Hardys were crossing the central courtyard on their way to the beach, Frank saw Fred Estival and waved to him. Estival changed course and joined them.

"Well," he said, brushing back a lock of black hair. "How are you enjoying the wonderful world of exploration?"

"I really liked the talk about satellite photos," Joe replied. "It gave me some ideas to try myself."

"You and a lot of others," Fred said with a laugh. "I'm almost glad I'm not at the Eriksson Foundation any longer. At least I won't have to wade through all the proposals that talk is bound to inspire."

He glanced up, and his face stiffened. Frank followed his gaze. Thor Sonderstrom had just come out onto an ornate stone balcony two flights up. He stood, gazing up at the sky, whistling to himself, apparently unaware of Fred and the Hardys in the courtyard below.

"Somebody's in for a lot of grief," Fred said softly. "I know that old buzzard better than he knows himself. When he whistles like that, it means he's made up his mind to shaft someone. I wonder who, not to mention why—"

"It really does look as if his mood has lightened," Joe remarked. "Maybe he found out who put that scorpion under his hat."

Fred nodded slowly. "I wish *I* knew who did it," he said with a bitter smile. "I'd like to shake his hand. Maybe he'd even lend me one of his scorpions. Now that I'm sure which is Thor's room, I could put it in his bed!"

After a couple of hours at the beach, the Hardys returned to their room, showered, and dressed for dinner. Downstairs, the reception room next to the state dining room was already crowded. A cheerful buzz of conversation filled the air. Joe and Frank accepted glasses of lemon-flavored mineral water from one of the waiters and joined Gail, Sally, and Doug.

"Have any of you been to one of these dinners before?" Joe asked.

Doug and Sally shook their heads.

"I have, lots of times," Gail said. "Daddy takes me whenever he can. They're really a lot of fun."

"Fried spiders with termite sauce?" Sally said with a little shiver. "No, thanks."

"Hardly anybody eats the really bizarre stuff," Gail told her. "It's basically there to give the media something to talk about. And some of the rest of it is actually pretty good. African antelope isn't that different from venison, and Peruvian peccary is just another kind of pork. Excuse me," she said, glancing behind her. "I think Daddy wants me."

She walked away. After a few moments Doug and Sally drifted over to the table of appetizers. Joe noticed Sonderstrom standing alone a few feet away. "Let's go talk to him," he murmured to Frank. "He must have some idea of who's out to get him."

They went over and said hello.

The foundation head stared at them blankly. Either he didn't recall who they were or his mind was totally occupied with something else.

"We're here as Perry Housman's guests," Frank reminded him. "Did you ever find out how that scorpion got under your hat this morning?"

Sonderstrom raised one eyebrow. "No, I'm afraid not," he said tonelessly. He shifted his gaze away from them as if to advise them their interview was over.

At that moment Robert Delaplane arrived, wearing a dapper tuxedo and carrying a goblet in each hand. He handed one to Sonderstrom and said, "I think the conference is going well. Don't you?"

Sonderstrom muttered noncommittally.

Joe said, "I've enjoyed all the presentations so far and learned a lot from them."

Sonderstrom and Delaplane both stared at him, then turned away without responding. Joe felt his cheeks grow warm. Frank touched his arm and gestured toward the table of appetizers.

Once they were a few feet away, Frank said, "What a couple of grouches! I've got half a mind to go hunting for a scorpion myself."

Gail and her father were standing nearby, so the Hardys joined them.

"Well, fellows, are you ready for the taste thrill of your lives?" Perry asked with a chuckle.

"We're not sure," Frank confessed. "Some of the things on the menu sound a little far out."

"Of course—that's the tradition. Food from the far corners of the world prepared by guild members who've been there," Perry replied.

"So guild people prepare all the dishes?" Joe asked.

Gail said, "It all depends. A lot of the recipes are pretty straightforward if you ignore the exotic ingredients. I mean, a roast is a roast. Any decent cook can take care of it. But some of the dishes call for special attention. A Brazilian anthropologist has been in the kitchen since he got here making a dessert from jungle fruit nobody even knows the name of."

"People take the dinner very seriously, don't they?" Frank remarked.

"It depends," Perry replied. "It's partly just for

fun. But a lot of our members really have gone to remote parts of the world and learned to like foods that might sound peculiar to the rest of us. Thor, for example, makes it a matter of pride to try almost anything once. Oops—here we go."

The crowd surged forward as the wide double doors swung open. Inside the dining room, Joe saw a row of long narrow tables along the left-hand wall covered with serving dishes. Each serving dish had a page next to it that identified its contents and explained where the dish came from. Joe, Frank, and their companions joined the line, just behind Doug and Sally.

"Wow!" Frank exclaimed. "Will you look at that clamshell? Do you suppose it's real? It must be at least two feet across!"

"It's a Pacific sea clam," Sally told him. "They get even bigger than that. But the really big ones are so tough that you'd be better off resoling your shoes with one than trying to eat it."

Just ahead of Doug, Fred was hesitating over a bowl of something orangy red. He finally moved on without taking any.

"What's that—do you know?" Joe asked Perry, pointing to the bowl.

Perry nodded. "That's a really interesting dish. It's a rare mushroom from Indonesia. Raw, they contain a powerful, deadly nerve toxin. But if you cook them the right way, they're supposed to be delicious."

"I think I'll pass," Joe said. As he did, he noticed Ahmed behind the table in a slightly overlarge waiter's uniform. Ahmed gave him a smile and a wink. Joe winked back before moving on to a platter of filleted perch from the river Nile. When he glanced back, he noticed that Sonderstrom, who was just behind Frank in line, was taking a heaping spoonful of the mushrooms.

The Hardys filled their plates and followed Perry and Gail to a table. Sonderstrom stopped next to them and asked Perry, "May I join you?"

"Of course," Perry said, surprised.

Sonderstrom sat down with a silent nod to the others.

Joe sampled a fried dumpling made from a kind of grain found only in the high Andes of South America. It tasted like a cross between a hush puppy and a fried wonton—okay, but nothing to write home about. With a shrug, he moved on to what was billed as roast zebu.

After one bite, he asked, "Does anybody know what kind of animal a zebu is?"

Gail grinned. "In the States, we call it a Brahma bull," she told him.

"No wonder it tastes like beef," Joe said, chuckling. "It is!"

Across the table, Sonderstrom gave Joe a disdainful look. Suddenly his face changed. His eyes bulged. His mouth opened, but no sound came out. He stiffened, tried to get to his feet, then fell to the table facedown.

Perry jumped up and ran over to him. He pulled him upright and felt for a pulse in his neck. After a moment he glanced around the table, his face white.

"He's dead," Perry said.

Chapter

6

THE NEWS SPREAD OUT through the room like ripples on the surface of a pond. As Frank and Joe joined Perry next to Sonderstrom's chair, a middle-aged man with a gray beard hurried over.

"Let me through, please," he said. "I'm a doctor."

He, too, felt Sonderstrom's neck, then lowered him to the floor. "Does anyone here know CPR?" he demanded, placing his joined hands on the unconscious man's chest and beginning to push rhythmically.

"My brother and I do," Frank told him. "Want us to take over?"

"Maybe later," the doctor replied. But after fifteen minutes, he rechecked Sonderstrom's pulse, then lifted one eyelid. With a shake of the head, he said, "I'm afraid there's nothing more to be done. We should notify the authorities immediately."

Perry glanced around at the silent crowd. "Would someone—"

Fred said, "I'll take care of it." He headed toward the doorway.

"What was it, Doctor?" Frank asked. "A heart attack?"

The doctor gave Frank a grim look. "I'm afraid not. In that case, we might have been able to save him. No, it looks to me as if he was suddenly paralyzed by some very powerful nerve toxin. In other words, I suspect poison!"

Joe's eyes widened. "The mushrooms," he gasped. "Don't let anybody else eat them!"

Perry instantly grasped Joe's point. He jumped up on a chair and shouted, "Attention, everybody. If you have the Indonesian mushrooms, *do not eat them.*"

Two tables away, a heavyset man heaved himself to his feet. "I already did," he wailed, his face turning green. He clapped his hand over his mouth and started for the exit.

"Now just hold on," somebody said in an authoritative voice. It was a tall man in horn-rimmed glasses.

"That's Paul Ferber. He's the one who fixed the mushrooms," Perry whispered to Frank and Joe.

"There's absolutely no cause for panic," Ferber continued. "I collected and cooked those mushrooms myself, and there's nothing wrong with them. I just finished a helping myself with no ill effects. Anybody else?"

The woman who had given the presentation on satellite imaging raised her hand. "I did, Paul. They were delicious. And I feel fine."

"I'm glad to hear it," Perry said. "I certainly didn't mean to cause a panic. But in any case, the authorities should be here soon, and I imagine they'd prefer nothing was disturbed."

Perry paused to speak in an undertone to one of the waiters, who left and returned with a large white tablecloth that he carefully draped over the dead man.

Just then two reporters and a photographer rushed in, barraging Perry with questions and snapping photos of the covered corpse. With the help of several other guild members, Perry managed to push them back out the door, telling them he'd have an official statement once he met with the authorities.

"Frank?" Joe said softly. "Are you thinking what I'm thinking?"

Frank nodded. "Somebody must have had a much bigger grudge against Sonderstrom than we thought. The skull and the scorpion were just warnings. Tonight was the main event in the program—murder!"

"It sure looks that way," Joe said. "But how?

You heard those people say that they ate the mushrooms without any effect."

Frank rubbed his cheek. "The murderer—if there was one—must have somehow arranged for Sonderstrom to get mushrooms that were still poisonous. Maybe he slipped them onto Sonderstrom's plate when he wasn't looking or put them in the serving dish with the harmless ones just before Sonderstrom took some."

"But how could the murderer know that Sonderstrom would take the mushrooms?" Joe protested. "Lots of people passed them up."

"Sure," Frank replied. "But don't you remember what Perry told us? Sonderstrom had a reputation for trying everything at these banquets. His killer must have known that."

Joe frowned. "That makes sense, but—" He broke off at the roar of angry voices. Following the sound, he saw Fred glaring at Robert Delaplane.

"I worked closely with Thor for years," Fred was saying. "Of course I'm sorry he's dead. As long as he was alive, there was always the chance that some miracle would turn him into a decent human being. But why should I try to pretend that it's the end of the world?"

"Your attitude shows a disgraceful lack of respect," Delaplane said.

"I lost my respect for Thor Sonderstrom years ago," Fred replied. "That's no secret. If you want to mouth phony praises, go ahead. But don't expect me to join in. And don't expect it to help you with future grants from the Leif Eriksson Foundation. I suspect a lot of board members feel the same way I did about Thor. Being a big friend of his probably won't buy you a whole lot."

Perry stepped in. "Robert, Fred—I know we're all upset by what just happened. But let's not say things we'll regret later."

Just then the dining-room door sprang open. Frank saw two uniformed men march in and stand on either side of the entrance. Next came two medics, one carrying a big medical kit, the other a folded stretcher. After a brief pause, three men in dark suits entered the room and stopped to survey the scene. Two were middle-aged, the third about thirty. He seemed to be in charge.

Perry went over, shook hands with the three men, and spoke to them briefly. Then he turned and said, "Ladies and gentlemen, I'd like to introduce Commissaire Meddour, of the Tunisian National Police. He'll be looking into this tragic event. I know you'll give him your full cooperation."

"Thank you," Meddour said in a crisp British accent. "I will not take any more of the time of our distinguished and honored guests than I must. There is a charming reception room next door. Perhaps you will wait there?"

The crowd began to move toward the door. Frank noticed that the uniformed officers were watching them closely. In the reception room, there were more police posted at the doors and windows. Commissaire Meddour might have a very polished public manner, but he wasn't taking any chances.

Joe glanced around, then asked softly, "Should we tell him what's been going on?"

Frank thought over the question. "If he asks, we ought to answer as truthfully as we can," he finally said. "But right now, all we really have are theories and suspicions, and I don't see the point in sharing them with him."

Another officer entered the reception room, scanned the crowd, and approached Perry. After a few low words, the two left the room.

"I wonder if there's some way I could hear what's going on in there," Joe said. "How about I tell the guy at the door that I'm going to the restroom? You distract him so that he doesn't notice how long I'm gone."

"I'll try," Frank promised.

Joe went up and spoke to the officer, then left the room. Frank waited a few minutes, then he, too, went over.

"Excuse me, Officer. Are you from around here?" he asked.

Confusion crossed the man's face. He glanced around the room, then said, "Ah, you mean from this town. Yes, sir, I am born here."

Frank gave him a big smile. "Terrific!" he said. "You see, while I'm here in Tunisia, I want to go somewhere to have a real Tunisian meal. It's great being a guest here at the palace, but somehow I don't have the sense that it's the real thing. You see what I mean?"

The officer scowled. For a moment Frank was afraid that he had somehow offended him. Then he realized that it was a scowl of concentration.

"If you please," the man said, "would you like to dine with my family tomorrow or the day after? My home is no palace, but you will see the real Tunisia there."

Frank suddenly felt ashamed. Here he was, trying to distract this man from doing his job, and in return he was offered hospitality.

"Thank you. I didn't mean—" he began.

The man pulled out a notebook and wrote on a blank page, tore it out, and offered it to Frank. "You do not have to decide," he said. "Here I have written my name, Said Kamal, and my telephone. Call tomorrow and say if you will come. I will tell my wife about this in case I am not home."

Frank put the sheet of paper in his shirt pocket, offered his hand, and said, "Thank you. I'm Frank Hardy." At that moment Joe returned and Frank introduced him to their prospective host. After the brothers had made plans to come to dinner in two days, the officer bid them a polite good evening.

"Did you find out anything?" Frank asked quietly as soon as they were alone.

"Nothing positive," Joe replied. "I managed to listen from behind a door while Meddour was questioning the waiters. As far as I could tell, nobody saw anything suspicious. I'm beginning to wonder—oops, here are Perry and Meddour now."

The buzz of conversation died down as the two men entered the room. When it was quiet, Commissaire Meddour said, "Thank you for your patience in these trying circumstances. We have finished our preliminary investigation. While the chemical analysis by our national crime laboratory will take several days to complete, it seems clear that Mr. Sonderstrom was the victim of a tragic accident."

"I protest!" Paul Ferber said loudly. "There was nothing harmful in those mushrooms."

"Now, Paul," Perry said, "don't get upset for nothing."

Ferber glared at him. "Nothing? They're saying I'm to blame for Sonderstrom's death!"

"Excuse me, Professor Ferber," Meddour said smoothly. "We are saying nothing of the sort. It is the opinion of our doctor that the deceased must have suffered a violent allergic reaction to something he ate. Perhaps the mushrooms or even some other food to which he was unaccustomed. In any case, no blame rests with those who prepared the food. As I said, a tragic accident. I hope you will not let your shock and sadness over it ruin your conference."

Perry had been conferring quietly with Delaplane. Now he stepped forward again and said, "I know Thor would have wanted us to go on. As you know, tonight was to be the inauguration of our new president. Under the circumstances, it seems more fitting to put that off until tomorrow. We'll have a special plenary session at ten. I hope you'll all be there. In the meantime, I'm afraid we'll have to forgo the rest of our banquet. However, the staff has very kindly agreed to prepare a light supper for us. It'll be served on the terrace in an hour."

As the crowd started to leave the room, Joe turned to Frank and said in a low voice, "What kind of investigation was that? They didn't even question anyone."

Frank frowned. "Once his doctor told him that Sonderstrom died accidentally, Meddour must have decided to put on the velvet gloves. This is a distinguished bunch of visitors, after all, from all over the world. No point in offending dozens of VIPs for nothing."

"Do you think it *was* an accident?" Joe demanded.

"After what happened yesterday and this morning? Of course not," Frank retorted. "But I don't think we'll get any movement from the authorities unless we turn up *proof* of a crime—proof they can't ignore."

"Then we're going on with our investigation?" Joe asked, relief in his voice.

Frank acted surprised. "Of course. Even if the cops are right about Sonderstrom having an allergic reaction, that doesn't explain the scorpion or the skull on his napkin. Someone was out to get him, and I want to know who."

Perry, walking by, overheard. He turned and said grimly, "Now listen, fellows. You heard what the man said. Thor's death was an accident."

"And the harassment?" Joe asked.

"Practical jokes," Perry said, his jaw tight. "Nasty ones, sure. But it's a long way from those to murder."

Frank said, "What if Sonderstrom's death was the result of a practical joke that went wrong? Don't you want to know who was responsible?"

"Frankly, no, I don't," Perry replied. "Sorry if that shocks you. But I have to think about the good of the Explorers Guild and the success of this conference. We've got journalists from all over the world covering this conference. In fact, I'm meeting with the press right now to explain what happened. A messy scandal could seriously damage the organization, and it won't do Thor any good. So just drop it, will you? If you can't find enough in the sessions to divert you, go see the sights or put in some time at the beach. But don't throw mud at the people who invited you here."

Frank felt a little like a kid being scolded for something he hadn't done. Was this the time to make a stand? he wondered.

Joe stood, scowling. His lips were pressed tight as if to say he didn't see the point in arguing.

In any case, they didn't have a chance to argue. Without waiting for their response, Perry walked away.

After a short silence, Joe said, "I still say we go ahead."

"I do, too," Frank replied. "But I can't say I'm happy about it. We are Perry's guests, after all. I wish he were on our side. Why does he want to discourage us?"

Joe shrugged. "I wish I knew. I hope it's for the reason he gave, to avoid a scandal. I'd hate to think it was anything—well, not to his credit. What now?"

Frank thought for a moment. "Maybe we should split up and question people. If those mushrooms were poisoned, somebody must have noticed something."

"Ahmed!" Joe exclaimed. "Remember? He was standing right there, on the other side of the buffet. I'm going to find him."

"Good idea," Frank said with a nod. "And I'll try to find out who was standing in back of Sonderstrom in line. He or she might have seen something important, maybe without even realizing it."

Joe headed in the direction of the kitchen. Frank checked out the reception room. Practically everyone had left, so he went into the wide corridor and walked toward the entrance hall. He paused there, deciding to see if anyone was in the courtyard. It seemed deserted, but as he neared the central fountain, a flicker of light caught his attention. He glanced upward. Just then, another flicker came from a window on the second floor. A window with a stone balcony outside it. He frowned. Wasn't that the balcony where he and Fred had seen Sonderstrom only a few hours before? Someone with a flashlight was searching the room.

Frank rushed inside and took the stairs three at a time, then crept down the hallway. The door to Sonderstrom's room was very slightly ajar. Frank pushed it open just enough to slip inside. He was reaching for the light switch when he heard a faint noise behind him. Before he could turn, someone jumped him and got a stranglehold on his throat.

Chapter

7

THE POWERFUL ARM STARTED to tighten around Frank's throat, cutting off his breath. He surged into action. Grasping his attacker's forearm with both hands, he fell suddenly to one knee and bent double. The attacker, taken by surprise, went flying over Frank's shoulder. As he crashed to the floor, Frank released his grip, sprang up, and groped for the light switch.

The ceiling light came on. Perry Housman was just stumbling to his feet. His fists were clenched and his face was twisted with anger. Head down like a taunted bull, he charged Frank. Frank braced himself to counter the attack. But suddenly Perry skidded to a halt and straightened up.

"Frank?" he said, confusion on his face. "What

are you doing here? This is Sonderstrom's room."

Was this a trick? Frank kept his guard up as he said, "I know that. I was down in the courtyard when I noticed somebody up here with a flashlight. So I came up to see who it was. But the minute I walked in, you tried to throttle me."

"I'm sorry about that," Perry said. Then, rubbing his shoulder, he added, "For more than one reason. What was that you used on me, jujitsu?"

"More or less," Frank replied, still on guard.

"Well, my story's a lot like yours," Perry continued. "I was on my way to talk to the media when I noticed a light up here and decided to investigate. The door was open when I got here, but the room was empty. Just then I heard somebody creeping along the hallway. I figured it might be the intruder coming back for something he'd forgotten. That's why I turned out the lights, then jumped you like that."

"I see," Frank said. Perry's explanation made sense—except Frank knew that the room light *hadn't been on.* So had Perry been standing around in the dark? Or had he been using the small but powerful flashlight that was not quite hidden in the back pocket of his pants?

Perry didn't seem to notice the reserve in Frank's voice. "As long as we're here, we'd better take a look around," Perry said. "But we shouldn't touch anything. Whoever was searching the place may have left fingerprints."

Frank was tempted to point out that every fairly intelligent criminal in the world knew about fingerprints and took precautions against leaving them. And, anyway, who was going to be up dusting for fingerprints? The police? Less than an hour before, Perry had been happy to hear that the investigation of Sonderstrom's death was going to be handled as quickly and quietly as possible. Was he now planning to tell Commissaire Meddour about the intruder in Sonderstrom's room and ask him to reopen the case? It didn't seem likely.

"Hey, look at this," Perry continued. "Someone's been going through Thor's papers."

Frank joined Perry at the ornate desk near the window. A handsome leather attaché case was sitting open on the corner of the desk. A dozen or more file folders were scattered across the top of the desk, their contents spilling out. Some of the papers had fallen to the floor.

"How can you be sure?" Frank asked. "Maybe Thor was just messy."

"No way," Perry replied firmly. "With him, everything was in place. The only paper you ever saw on his desk was the one he was working on at the moment. Everything else was filed away. I'm sure someone was searching this stuff, and he was in a big hurry to find what he wanted."

Frank stood for a moment, surveying the scene. There were still four or five folders in the attaché case, apparently untouched. Why? Had the intruder left them because he heard someone coming and had to break off his search? Or had he finally found what he was looking for?

One of the papers on the desk caught Frank's eye. It was a copy of the minutes of an Eriksson Foundation board meeting. The date was only a few days earlier. The third item was a list of grant proposals that the board had voted on. Scanning it quickly, Frank spotted the names of Doug Rourk, Sally Komatsu, and Robert Delaplane, who'd had their funding requests approved. Had they heard the good news? Frank doubted it. All of them seemed too anxious to be aware of the decision.

Sonderstrom had obviously been going over the minutes carefully. There were a number of notes and corrections scribbled in the margin in red ink. As for the grant recipients, some were circled, some had question marks next to them, and a few were indicated with arrows. Sally's was one of the arrowed names, while Doug had a question mark next to his, and Delaplane's name was boldly circled.

"There's no way to tell if anything's missing," Perry remarked. "I feel funny looking at this stuff. I imagine a lot of it's confidential. What we ought to do is pack it up and send it back to the Eriksson Foundation. Too bad Fred Estival isn't with the outfit anymore. I could ask him to take care of it."

Frank slowly walked around the room, searching it for clues, but he didn't notice anything out of the ordinary. "Fred worked for the foundation a long time, didn't he?" he asked Perry. "Did Sonderstrom ever tell you why he was fired?"

Perry shook his head. "Not in so many words. But I got the feeling that Fred wasn't as responsible as he should have been in financial matters. Thor hinted that he did Fred a big favor when he simply let him go instead of taking the proof he had to the authorities."

"Proof? You mean, of criminal activities?" Frank pursued. "Embezzlement? Theft?"

Perry acted embarrassed. "Look, Frank, let's forget it. I shouldn't have opened my mouth. I like Fred, and I don't for a minute believe he's a crook. Now let's get out of here and be sure the door locks behind us."

As Frank followed Perry downstairs, a whole series of questions ran through his mind. Had Sonderstrom really had evidence that would convict Fred Estival of a crime? Had he brought it with him to this conference in order to confront Fred with it? If so, was it Fred who had searched Sonderstrom's room just now, hoping to find and destroy the evidence? More upsetting still, was it possible that Fred had murdered Sonderstrom to keep him from taking that evidence to the authorities?

Downstairs in the entry hall, Perry turned and said, "I'm going to see where we stand with supper. And then I've got to face the press. They're probably already hounding any guild member they can find for answers."

"I'll come with you," Frank replied. For a minute it seemed as if Perry was going to object, but he just shrugged and headed into the corridor.

Frank followed him past the dining room, through an inconspicuous door, and down a long hallway to the kitchen. It was huge, with high ceilings and tiled walls. On a big table in the center of the room, half a dozen men in white aprons were hurriedly assembling platters of sandwiches, bowls of fruit, and plates of relishes. One man who had his back to them was using toothpicks to pin olives, pickles, and rolled pieces of ham and turkey to a whole pineapple.

An older man in a dark jacket noticed Perry and Frank and rushed over. "Five minutes, sir," he said. "I apologize for the delay. We could not work in the kitchen until the police had finished."

"No apologies needed," Perry said. "I'm just glad you could do anything at all for us under these terrible circumstances."

Waiters began to carry the trays out to the terrace. Ahmed was one of them. He gave Frank a nod as he passed.

Frank and Perry followed the waiters outside. The terrace was lit by torches on tall poles. The flames flickered and twisted in the breeze from the sea. The conference participants were standing in little groups, talking quietly among themselves. Most of them had the dazed look of survivors after a tragedy. A radio reporter with a cassette recorder in her hand was interviewing Robert Delaplane. As Frank passed, he heard Delaplane saying, "A great loss to the world of exploration."

Frank spotted Joe off to one side by himself. He joined him.

"I wonder if we're moving in the wrong direction," Joe began, obviously frustrated. "Ahmed was standing behind the table practically all the time, and he swears he didn't see anybody put anything in those mushrooms."

"The culprit would have done his best not to be seen," Frank pointed out. "And even if it turns out that Sonderstrom's death really was an accident, *something* is going on around here." He told Joe about the intruder in Sonderstrom's room.

"Do you think it was Perry?" Joe asked.

Frank sighed. "It could be. He was on the scene, and he had a flashlight with him. Whoever it was, I'd like to know what he was after."

"Something he expected to find among Sonderstrom's papers," Joe said. "But since we don't know everything there was in those papers, it's going to be hard to know what it might have been."

"Well, I did learn a couple of things," Frank said. He filled Joe in about the grant approvals and Perry's suggestion that Fred had been fired because of alleged shady financial dealings.

"If it's true, that makes Fred a major suspect," Joe said thoughtfully. "But not the only one. Sally had the best opportunity to draw the skull on Sonderstrom's napkin. And I hate to say it, but we ought to keep an eye on Perry. I don't like the way he tried to pull us off the case or the fact that you found him in Sonderstrom's room just now."

The crowd began to move toward the buffet. Frank and Joe joined the line. Frank shivered when he noticed Fred several people ahead of him. It was almost a repetition of the scene earlier in the evening, just before Sonderstrom died.

By the time the Hardys finished serving themselves, Fred was already seated at a table for four near the edge of the terrace. He beckoned to them to join him. "I hope you don't mind eating with an outcast," he said lightly as they sat down.

"What do you mean?" Frank asked.

"That argument I had with Delaplane this evening," Fred replied. "Three or four people have let me know that I shouldn't have criticized Thor like that. The funny part is, yesterday one of those same people called Thor an egotistical monster. Which he was, of course. But now that he's dead, we're not supposed to mention his faults. What a bunch of hypocrites."

"Was he a good administrator?" Joe asked.

Fred considered the question. "He was well

organized, I have to give him that. But he didn't know how to delegate responsibility. He wasn't comfortable unless he was totally in charge. I'll give you an example. Ordinarily, an executive secretary at an outfit like Eriksson would have been preparing budgets, okaying expenditures, and generally handling the day-to-day operations so that the president could focus on policy issues. But not with Thor in charge. Even the smallest requisition had to have his okay. And he didn't rubber-stamp them either. One time we had a major fight over the price we were paying for ballpoint pens and memo pads."

"So the organization's finances were totally under his control?" Frank asked.

"That's right," Fred replied. "But that's not the point. *Everything* was—grant approvals, hiring and firing, expense accounts ... Frankly, I don't know how he found the time to do it all."

"You said earlier that he sometimes turned down grants even after they'd been approved by the board," Frank said. "How could he do that?"

Fred laughed bitterly. "Simple. The motions the board voted on were always made conditional to his consent. That gave him the power to override. And he used it, too. One of his big thrills was going over the list of approved grant applications and deciding which ones he was going to let stand. He'd mark them up with a red pen. Now and then he circled somebody's name. That meant he definitely wanted to fund the project. If he put a question mark next to it, that obviously meant he wasn't sure. But if he marked it with an arrow, look out! That meant he was planning to ax the grant."

Frank remembered the marked-up minutes. So Sonderstrom had been planning to override Sally's grant approval and was thinking about doing the same to Doug's.

"How many people knew about his habit of marking the minutes?" Frank asked Fred.

"Oh, lots of people," Fred replied. "We used to make jokes about it in the office—though not when Thor was around, of course."

Joe asked, "What will happen to grants that have been approved now that Sonderstrom is dead?"

Fred shrugged. "I'm sure that whatever the board decided will stand. Nobody but Sonderstrom had the authority to override the decisions."

Frank glanced across the table and met Joe's eyes. He saw that Joe was thinking the same thing. Fred didn't know it, but he had just told them that Sally Komatsu had a powerful motive for killing Thor Sonderstrom and that Doug Rourk's was almost as strong.

Chapter

8

FRED DIDN'T SEEM to notice the exchange between Frank and Joe. He finished his sandwich and said, "I'm going back for seconds. Do either of you want anything?"

"No, thanks. Not yet," Joe said, replying for both of them. As soon as Fred left the table, he spoke to Frank, lowering his voice. "Did you hear that? Sonderstrom was planning to cancel Sally's grant even though the foundation had approved it."

"And he had questions about Doug's grant, too," Frank replied. "Their projects are the most important things in the world to them. They'd do almost anything to make sure they were funded."

Joe nodded soberly. "And now, with Sonderstrom dead, they don't have to worry about their grants being canceled."

Frank frowned. "That's assuming that Sally knew she'd gotten the grant *and* that Sonderstrom was planning to ax it. And the same for Doug. Otherwise, neither of them had any reason to want to harass Sonderstrom, never mind kill him."

"That's true," Joe said. "But what if one or the other of them found out somehow?"

"How?" Frank insisted. "If one of them got a look at Sonderstrom's papers and knew what his marks meant, okay. But whoever searched Sonderstrom's room did it after he was dead. There's no way that anything that was found out could have been the motive for killing him."

"Logic, always logic," Joe joked. "So they found out some other way. Gossip, rumors, reading tea leaves . . ."

Fred returned with his plate heaped high. "I don't know why I'm so hungry," he said gloomily. "Maybe because I don't know where my next meal is coming from."

"Are things really that bad?" Frank asked.

"Yes and no," he replied. "My training is pretty specialized—classical Greek archeology. University jobs in my field open up only when somebody retires or dies. I can't count on that happening before my savings run out."

"How did you end up doing administrative work at the Eriksson Foundation?" Frank asked.

Fred shrugged. "Partly accident. I was originally hired as a program officer for archeology. I did some streamlining of procedures that caught Thor's attention, and he asked me to become executive secretary. But if I'd known how little responsibility he'd end up giving me, I probably would have said no."

"There must be other foundations that could use somebody with your experience," Joe suggested.

"I hope so," Fred said. "On the other hand, I'm not sure I want to spend the rest of my life being a paper shuffler."

"Suppose somebody applies for a grant," Frank said after a pause. "How does she find out if her project has been approved?" he asked.

Fred seemed a little surprised at the abrupt change of subject, but he answered, "Most granting agencies try to let people know as quickly as possible. The project leaders have to make plans, after all. Some grants officers will even notify applicants by phone, then send a formal letter of confirmation later. I would have liked to work that way myself. Why keep people in suspense?" He sighed and went on. "But, of course, at Eriksson it didn't work that way. All funding decisions were only made public by Thor Sonderstrom. Until he made up his mind and let the applicant know, we weren't even supposed to hint at the outcome."

"What about rumors?" Joe asked.

Fred rolled his eyes. "There's no escaping them. And there's no way to stop people from second-guessing the foundation's decisions. Have you heard what happened to Portago, the gorilla expert?"

"Yes, you told me yesterday," Frank said. "Whatever became of him?"

"Portago? I don't know," Fred confessed. "I wish I did. If I'd been in his place, I would have been tempted to go after Thor Sonderstrom with a horsewhip."

Or a poisoned mushroom? Frank thought. What if Portago were at the conference in disguise? Aloud he asked, "Did you ever meet him?"

"Sure," Fred replied. "He came to lunch at the foundation one time. I was really impressed by the way he managed with just one hand."

"One hand?" Frank repeated.

Fred nodded. "That's right. He lost his left hand a few years ago. A minor wound became infected while he was in the field, days from the nearest hospital. By the time he got medical help, there was nothing to do but amputate."

He took a long drink of his soda. When he put down the glass, his face was tired and drawn. "I'm beat," he said. "I guess seeing somebody you've known for years fall dead takes it out of you—even if you didn't like the person much. I'm going to turn in. See you tomorrow."

His step was unsteady as he left the terrace.

Frank watched, then turned to Joe. "Well, so much for the idea that Portago might be here in disguise. There's no one at the conference who's missing a hand or wearing an artificial one. And if Fred was telling us the truth about the way the Eriksson Foundation works, then the motive we thought he had didn't exist," he said.

"Some kind of financial funny business, you mean?" Joe asked. "I don't follow you."

Frank said, "If Sonderstrom was such a power freak that he didn't let anybody else have real responsibility, then I don't see how Fred could have managed to pull anything shady. And Fred had to be telling us something close to the truth about the way Sonderstrom managed the foundation. Too many other people know the facts, too."

Joe seemed uncomfortable. "In other words, we cross him off our list of suspects?"

"I didn't say that," Frank retorted. "But I don't think we should focus all our attention on him either. If you ask me, both Sally and Doug are as high on the list as Fred. If either of them got a look at those board minutes and knew what Sonderstrom's marks meant, that'd give him or her a solid motive to get rid of Sonderstrom before he axed their grants. I think both of them deserve a closer look."

Joe glanced around. "There's Sally over there, talking to Delaplane," he said, getting to his feet. "I'll see if I can horn in."

"Okay," Frank said. "And I'll find Doug. What we need to know is if either of them knew about the board's decision on their grants and how to decipher Sonderstrom's red marks. Let's meet back here in half an hour to compare notes."

As Joe was crossing the terrace, Gail called his name and motioned for him to join her. She was sitting alone at a table, her salad and sandwiches untouched. After a moment's hesitation, Joe went over and sat down in a chair that allowed him to watch Sally and Delaplane.

"Aren't you hungry?" he asked.

Gail shook her head. "Every time I think about eating something, I start wondering if I might have some weird allergy."

"You have to eat," Joe said sensibly. "Just stay away from strange mushrooms."

"I don't think the mushrooms had anything to do with it," Gail said, giving him a sidelong glance. "Look at all the other people who ate them without any problem."

"True," Joe said, keeping an eye on Sally. She looked a lot less tense than she had earlier. As she talked to Delaplane, she smiled and lightly touched his arm. Joe wished he could hear what they were saying.

Gail followed the direction of his glance. "Poor Sally," she said.

Joe looked at her in surprise. "Why?"

Gail rolled her eyes. "Haven't you noticed? She's spending every minute talking to every influential person at the conference. I was there when she glommed on to my dad. It was obvious she was after him to help her raise money for her project. It's too bad she can't stick to her underwater work and let somebody else sell the project for her."

"I never realized how important foundations are for this kind of work," Joe said. "People like Sonderstrom, who have to choose among different projects, must make enemies right and left. I wonder which of Sonderstrom's enemies put that scorpion under his hat this morning?"

Gail became very still for a moment, then said, "I don't even want to talk about it. I hate those things. When I was at camp in Colorado a couple of years ago, we had to shake out our shoes every morning before putting them on just in case a scorpion had moved in. The idea made me so sick, I could barely eat breakfast."

Joe smiled sympathetically. "And did you ever find one in your shoe?"

"No, but one of my tentmates did," Gail replied. "I almost died on the spot."

Joe shook his head, only half listening. Sally had just glanced at her watch and given Delaplane a smile before heading along the terrace and down the steps to the garden. In another moment she'd be out of sight.

Joe stood up. "Sorry," he said to Gail. "I just

remembered something I have to do. See you later."

Joe reached the edge of the terrace just in time to see Sally step off the path into the bushes. He hurried to the spot where he had last seen her. She seemed to be heading for the beach.

"Have you started work on your next film yet?" Frank asked Doug.

"Hmmm?" Doug said absently. He glanced at his wrist, then around the terrace before focusing on Frank. "Oh—not exactly. I'm still trying to raise money for it."

Frank nodded sympathetically. "Everybody says how hard that is."

"Believe it," Doug said with a bitter laugh. "I thought it would get easier after my first film. No way. If something doesn't work soon, I'm going to have to go back to shooting commercials—unless I shoot myself first."

As Frank started to reply, Doug glanced at his watch again. "I'll catch you later, okay?" Without waiting for Frank's response, he quickly moved into the garden. Frank let him get a little ahead, then followed.

A three-quarter moon rode low over the ocean. Its light made the shadows even deeper. Frank narrowed his eyes and strained to keep Doug in sight. Where was he going?

For a moment the white oval of Doug's face appeared as he peeked back over his shoulder.

Frank quickly stepped off the path into the bushes. Holding his hands out to protect his face, he started to tiptoe through the shrubbery, parallel to the path. Ahead, through the leaves, he could see the white sand of the beach and the glimmer of moonlight on the water. He was about to step out of the bushes onto the beach when he sensed something moving to his left. He whirled just in time to see a tall figure rush at him out of the darkness, arms spread wide to attack.

Chapter

9

As THE UNKNOWN ATTACKER swooped down on him, Frank's reflexes took over. He made a feint to the left, then grabbed his opponent's arm, spun on his heel, and used his opponent's forward momentum to throw the attacker over his shoulder. It almost worked the way he intended, but Frank hadn't counted on his attacker grabbing his belt. As the attacker flipped over Frank's back, Frank was pulled down with him.

As he felt himself fall, Frank tucked his head before he hit the ground and rolled. He sprang up just in time to deflect a right aimed at his face. He grasped the arm and tried for another shoulder throw, but his opponent knew the response to that move. A moment later Frank was tossed and facedown on the ground with a knee grinding into his back. He had a grip on his opponent's right hand. Desperate, he began to bend the man's fingers backward.

There was an explosion of air near his left ear as his opponent groaned, rolled off Frank, and jerked his hand from Frank's grasp. Frank rolled in the opposite direction and pushed himself to his feet again, ready for the next attack. Who was this guy? Obviously someone with at least as much martial arts training as Frank. And much the same training, too. In fact, his moves had an eerie resemblance to Frank's own, as if he were fighting his mirror image. Or—

"Joe?" Frank whispered as his opponent came at him again.

In the darkness Frank could hear the other shape skid to a halt. "Frank? Is that you?"

Frank straightened up. "Who did you think it was?" he returned, rubbing his back. "That knee of yours is sharp. How'd you get so fast?"

"Practice, practice," Joe replied. "I thought you were going to break my fingers."

"I would have if that's what it took to get you off me," Frank admitted. "What are you doing here?"

"Following Sally," Joe replied. "What are *you* doing here?"

"Following Doug," Frank said. "Something tells me they're meeting each other."

Joe said, "Of course! They must be in it together. I had a feeling one person couldn't have been responsible for everything that's happened."

"Come on," Frank said. "With any luck, we can get close enough to hear what they're saying."

Frank led the way through the bushes toward the beach, with Joe close behind. The moon cast a faint path of light across the water and illuminated the beach, casting the figures of Sally and Doug into silhouette.

Frank stopped just before he reached the sand and held out an arm to keep Joe from going any farther. Doug and Sally were only a dozen feet away, close enough for Frank and Joe to hear every word they spoke. They weren't talking, though. They were facing each other with their hands joined. As they moved toward each other in the moonlight and began to kiss, with the soft lapping of the surf in the background, Frank felt his face redden. He and Joe had no business spying on them like this. He gave Joe a shove and retreated into the bushes after him.

"I think we misread the situation," he muttered as soon as he and Joe were farther away. "It doesn't look like they're plotting anything. Let's get back to the palace before they realize we're here and jump to the wrong conclusion about *us*."

Joe was the first one up the next morning. He folded back the wooden shutters. The day was already bright with a beautiful clear sky. He took a deep breath. Along with a tang of the sea, the breeze carried the aroma of fresh-brewed coffee and baked bread.

On his way to the bathroom, Joe threw a pillow in the direction of Frank's head. "Come on, lazy," he said. "Rise and shine, it's breakfast time."

Frank hurled the pillow back with deadly aim.

Once dressed, the Hardys went downstairs to the terrace. The breakfast buffet was set up, and people filled their plates and took them to tables. A few minutes later Gail came over.

"May I join you?" she asked.

Frank sprang up and pulled out a chair for her. "Sure," he said with a warm smile.

"I could hardly sleep last night, I was so upset about Thor," Gail said. "Not that he was a particularly good friend, but I'd known him ever since Daddy started bringing me to these meetings. You don't expect to see somebody you know drop dead like that."

Frank was putting jam on a slice of French bread. He paused to say, "It must have been a shock for a lot of people."

"I just hope it won't ruin the conference," Gail continued.

Hans came over and sat down with them. As he was greeting Gail and the Hardys, there was a crackle of static from the public address system.

Joe looked around. Perry was standing near the buffet with a mike in his hand. "If I could have your attention?" he said. "Bob Delaplane and I had a discussion last night about the conference schedule. We've decided to postpone his inauguration as president of the guild until this evening's session, but the rest of today's schedule remains as planned. So this morning at ten, there'll be buses out front to take us to El Djem. We'll have lunch there and be back in plenty of time for Eleanor Coleman's presentation about reintroducing timber wolves to the forests of New England. Oh, and don't forget there's an official reception at five at the castle in the middle of town. I'm sure you've all seen it. It's important that we all be there out of courtesy to our hosts. Okay, that's all."

"I have never heard of this El Djem," Hans said. "Why are we going there?"

"It sounds fascinating," Gail replied, tapping her guidebook. "These days, El Djem is just a village in the middle of nowhere, but two thousand years ago, it was a wealthy and important city. The olive oil capital of the Roman Empire as a matter of fact."

"The Roman Empire? But we're in North Africa," Joe said.

Gail explained, "The Roman Empire stretched all the way from England almost to India. This part, what's now Tunisia, was practically in the center of everything. Anyway, to show how rich and important their city was, the people of El Djem built a coliseum that was almost as big as the one in Rome. People came from all over North Africa for the games. And the coliseum is still there, mostly intact."

"What happened to the city?" Joe asked. "Why isn't *it* still there?"

"Apparently there was a big fight about who would be the next emperor, and El Djem backed the wrong guy," Gail replied. "Then later, the climate got drier, the desert moved in, and the olive groves died, so there was no more need for a city."

"It's strange to think," Hans said, "that in two thousand years people may talk of Vienna or New York as we are talking about El Djem."

Gail shivered. "Don't!" she said. "That gives me a really creepy feeling. Let's talk about something else."

Frank jumped in. "Yesterday Joe and I met a guy on the beach who was giving camel rides. I hope we find time to take one while we're here."

Gail laughed. "The guy who named his camels Brigitte and Gina, you mean? I'd love to try that, too. Let's make a date. We can take turns riding the camels and snapping pictures to show our friends back home."

"Great idea," Frank said, giving her a warm look.

Joe fished his schedule from his back pocket. "There's no time today," he said after studying it. "What about right after breakfast tomorrow?"

"You're on," Gail replied. She glanced at her

watch. "Hey, we'd better finish eating. The buses are leaving in fifteen minutes."

South of the palace the road led between groves of silver-gray olive trees. Occasionally, tall date palms marked the site of a house with white walls and a roof of red tiles. Frank nudged Joe and pointed out a man who was filling big water jugs at a roadside well while his donkey waited patiently to carry them home.

Gradually the landscape changed. The olive trees became scarcer, and between the occasional groves were stretches of reddish rock-strewn sand where only cactus and low scrub grew.

The bus topped a low rise and followed the curve of the road to the left. Joe's eyes widened. "Frank," he exclaimed. "Look at that!"

Far on the horizon, an improbably huge structure loomed against the blue desert sky. "That must be the coliseum," Joe added. "I never imagined it would be so big."

Soon the bus entered the small, dusty village and followed a narrow, winding street to a plaza in front of the coliseum. Once off the bus, Joe paused and craned his neck to stare up at the three levels of arched openings in the honey-colored stone. It looked as if, after two thousand years, every stone was still in place.

"Excuse us, please," a familiar voice said. Ahmed was grinning up at him. In his arms were stacks of metal food containers. Behind him, other members of the palace staff were unloading folding tables, drink coolers, and boxes of supplies from the baggage compartment of the bus. Joe returned the boy's grin and stepped out of the way. Then he and Frank made their way through a crowd of souvenir peddlers to the entrance.

Perry saw them coming and waited. "Pretty amazing, isn't it?" he said.

Inside the entrance, they found themselves in a wide, curving corridor with an arched stone ceiling. By contrast with the glaring light outside, it was almost gloomy. To the left, a stone stairway led up to the next level, and a little farther along, the corridor was blocked by a wooden barrier.

Stone-floor passages led from the corridor to the interior of the arena. When Joe and Frank followed the nearest one, Joe was surprised to see that the center of the arena was a maze of corridors bordered by high stone walls. He turned and gazed upward at level after level of stone ramps that circled the stadium. "Where did the people sit?" he asked.

"On wooden benches," Perry replied. "Long gone, of course. And those passages in the center were originally under the floor of the arena. That's where they kept the gladiators and wild animals until their turns to come out."

"I wonder how many spectators it held," Frank said.

Gail joined them in time to hear the question. "Over thirty thousand," she told him. "Can you imagine that many people here?"

With Perry and Gail, the Hardys explored the center of the arena, stepping over fallen blocks of stone as they went. Though the other people from the conference were doing the same thing, the coliseum was so huge that they had the sense of being alone.

"I want to see what it's like from the top level," Joe declared after a while. "What about the rest of you?"

Frank agreed, but Gail and Perry decided to explore the lower level. It was a long, tiring climb. The stone steps were steep and uneven, calling for careful navigating. Finally at the top level, they found, as on the levels below, a corridor that circled the coliseum. The arched openings offered a view out over the surrounding countryside. On the other side of the corridor, a short flight of steps took them onto a stone platform that overlooked the arena, seventy-five feet below. Stray blocks of stone that ranged in size from a shoebox to a TV set dotted the platform.

Joe walked to within a few inches of the edge. There was no guardrail. He peered over and tried to imagine how the arena had looked two thousand years before, filled with cheering spectators, but something kept distracting him. Finally he identified what it was. "I smell hamburgers," he announced.

"It *is* close to lunchtime," Frank replied. "Let's go back down and check out the food."

At ground level they found serving tables set up along one wall of the roofed corridor. Just outside, but still in the shade, one of the staff was grilling meat on a charcoal fire. Joe and Frank joined the line.

Ahmed was passing out plates and cutlery. When Joe and Frank reached him, he grinned and said, "See what I have."

He held up a glass jar. Inside was a live scorpion.

Frank just stared at it. "Ahmed, where did you get that?" he demanded.

"I caught it," Ahmed said proudly. "There is an old man in the *souk* who buys them to make into powder for medicine. But the last one I caught someone stole from me."

"When was that, Ahmed? And where?" Joe asked.

The urgency in Joe's voice made the boy draw back a little. But after a brief hesitation, he said, "It was the day you came. You remember, I took you on a tour. And later, some of your friends wanted to see the kitchen. I kept the jar with the scorpion in a secret place at the back of the big pantry. The next morning I saw it was gone."

"Which friends, Ahmed?" asked Frank.

"Mister Spaceman and his daughter and the woman from Japan," Ahmed answered.

Joe realized he meant Perry, Gail, and Sally. "Why didn't you say anything about losing your scorpion?" he asked, dismayed.

Ahmed hesitated again. "I was afraid to get in trouble for keeping one at all. But this one I will not lose, I promise."

"Thanks, Ahmed," Frank said. "And good luck catching more scorpions."

"Let's find Gail," Frank muttered. "I'd like to know more about that kitchen tour."

Gail was waiting at the end of the serving line. "Sure, we saw Ahmed's scorpion," she said in reply to Frank's question. "I didn't look too closely. I told you how much I hate those things."

"Did you all stay together afterward?" Joe asked.

"Well, sure," Gail replied. "Sally went back for a glass of water, but she came right out again."

Frank asked, "Was she carrying a handbag?"

Gail gave him a puzzled look. "Sure. Why?"

"Ahmed's scorpion vanished sometime between your visit and the next morning," Frank explained. "And at breakfast there was a scorpion under Thor Sonderstrom's hat."

"You don't really suspect Sally, do you?" Gail demanded.

"Well, somebody did it," Joe pointed out. "Somebody with access to a live scorpion, which looks like the same thing as someone with access to the kitchen and Ahmed's scorpion."

"I see your point," Gail said. Her face turned pale, and she swayed on her feet. "Excuse me, I think the heat must be getting to me. I'm going to sit down."

"Can I help?" Frank asked quickly.

"No, don't bother. I'll be all right in a minute." She walked away slowly.

"What now?" Joe asked. "Do we go looking for Sally?"

"I think we'd better eat something first," Frank replied. "No telling how long they'll keep serving."

A few minutes later Joe and Frank were sitting on a fallen pillar at the edge of the arena, balancing plates on their knees.

"I wonder what kind of spice they put in the hamburgers," Joe said. "I think I like it."

"Wait'll you try the grilled shrimp," Frank replied. "They're terrific. But watch out for the red sauce—it's pure fire. After one taste, I had to finish all my ice water."

Joe was about to make a joke when he heard a shout. "Heads up! Look out!"

Joe threw his head back to look up. A block of stone was just falling over the edge of the upper level of the coliseum. He and Frank were directly beneath it.

Chapter

10

FRANK DIDN'T TAKE the time to shout but gave his brother a shove as the heavy block of stone plummeted down toward them.

Joe dived to the left. Frank threw himself to the right and did a forward roll. When he got to his feet, he had his arms wrapped around his head for protection.

The block of stone hit the pillar, right where they'd been sitting. Fragments of rock showered Frank. One, sharper than the others, nicked his wrist. He ignored the pain.

"Joe?" he said urgently. "Are you okay?"

Joe, too, was on his feet, shading his eyes with his hand and staring upward. "Yeah," he said.

"Whoever tried to pulverize us must still be up there," Frank replied. "Come on, let's get him."

They sprinted through the gathering crowd, brushing aside the questions that were posed as they passed. In the corridor, there were stairways to the upper levels in each direction. Joe ran toward the one on the right, while Frank took the one on the left.

Frank was halfway up the second flight of stairs when he saw Sally coming down. He thrust out an arm to stop her and demanded, "What are you doing here?"

She raised her eyebrows and said, "I heard shouting. What's going on?"

Frank didn't reply. He could question her later. Pushing past, he continued to dash up the stairs. When he reached the top level, he had to pause to catch his breath. At that moment Joe appeared at the head of the other stairs and came toward him.

"Anything?" Joe asked, panting.

Frank shook his head. "On my way up, I passed Sally," he reported. "No one else, though." With his hands on his hips, he turned to scan the area. There were lots of loose blocks of stone scattered around, but no place for anyone to hide.

"I didn't see anybody on my way up," Joe said. "Either that block just happened to fall—"

"Or Sally pushed it," Frank said. "I know. She could have overheard us talking to Ahmed or Gail and realized we were closing in on her. Did you get a good look at the stone? How big would you say it was?"

"When it was falling, it appeared as large as a truck," Joe said. "But the truth is, it wasn't much bigger than two dictionaries tied together."

Frank scanned the area until he found a block of stone about the same size, then tried to lift it. It was heavy, but when he slid it or tipped it up end over end, he could move it without much difficulty. "I think Sally could have managed one this size," he reported. "But we'd better eliminate the possibility of an accident."

He and Joe approached the edge and looked down. A crowd was gathered around the spot where they had been sitting. Many of the people were staring upward.

"It looks like it came from about twenty feet to the left," Frank estimated. As he and Joe drew near the spot, they made a wide circle, carefully studying the sandy stone floor before they stepped on it.

"See those scratch marks in the sand?" Joe said, pointing. "They look fresh. Somebody slid that stone block to the edge and shoved it over the side. So much for an accident."

Frank got down on his hands and knees and bent over until his cheek almost touched the stone floor. The acute angle made the marks show up much more clearly. "I see some marks that could be footprints," he told Joe. "But they're much too blurry to be of any help. That's odd—the surface of the stone is darker at the edge."

He crept over and looked at the spot closely, then put his palm down on it. "It's damp," he reported. "I wonder why? I wouldn't think anything would stay damp for long in air so hot and dry."

"Damp, dry—what does it matter?" Joe demanded. "We know who tried to turn us into jelly with that block of stone. And we have a pretty good idea of why, too. It's time we had a talk with Sally."

Frank took another minute or two to study the stone floor but finally had to admit there was nothing else for him to learn. He straightened up and followed Joe down the stairs.

At the bottom, Perry came hurrying over. "Are you boys all right?" he demanded. "That was a close call. They ought to do more to stabilize this structure before someone is killed."

This wasn't the moment to explain that the stone hadn't fallen accidentally. Frank scanned the crowd. Sally was on the far side with Doug, her back to the Hardys. Was the couple simply involved in a romance or in conspiracy as well?

Frank and Joe moved grimly toward Sally. Doug noticed them coming and frowned. Sally must have seen his expression because she turned around.

"Frank, your hand is bleeding," she said.

"It could have been worse," Frank replied.

"Don't neglect it," Sally continued. "I wonder if there's a first-aid kit in the bus? I'll go ask."

"Thanks, but it can wait," Frank said. "Can we talk to you for a minute? Privately?"

"I guess so," she replied, sounding puzzled and alarmed.

"I'll see you later," Doug said with a frown, and walked away.

Frank led the way to a deserted corner of a nearby passage.

"What's up?" Sally asked. "You two look awfully serious."

"We've been trying to find out who was harassing Sonderstrom," Joe said. "And I think we must be getting close, because somebody just tried to kill us."

"How awful!" Sally exclaimed. "Who?"

Frank skirted her question. "You remember when we were touring the palace the other day? Why did you leave us and go back to the dining room?"

Sally's cheeks reddened. "I told you, to get my camera," she said.

"And later on, when Ahmed was showing you around the kitchen," Joe said, "you made an excuse to go back inside then, too."

"What do you mean, excuse? I was thirsty and went back to get a glass of water," she said, her voice rising. "Listen, I don't like your insinuations. And I don't have to answer any more of your questions."

With that, she started to walk away.

Frank said, "Sally? Did you know that someone took Ahmed's scorpion from the kitchen after your tour?"

Sally turned back to him with what appeared to be genuine puzzlement. "Really?" Her expression changed. "You guys think I put that nightmarish thing under Thor Sonderstrom's hat? That's crazy! Why on earth would I want to pull a dirty trick on the president of the Leif Eriksson Foundation? I was doing my best to get on his good side."

Frank hid his unease. All along, this had been the weakest link in their case against Sally. It still was. "You could have been hoping to make him suspicious of someone else," he said. "If you kept him off balance, maybe he wouldn't cancel your grant."

"You're way off," Sally declared. "I don't even *have* a grant from the Eriksson Foundation, not yet anyway. So how could Thor Sonderstrom have canceled it?"

She stopped suddenly and studied Frank's face carefully. "You wouldn't by any chance know something I don't know, would you?" she demanded.

Frank did his best to keep a poker face, but it clearly didn't work.

Sally's eyes lit up. "You do! They approved my proposal!"

"Yeah, but Sonderstrom was planning to ax

it," Joe said. "Maybe when you found that out, you decided to do whatever you had to to stop him."

"Cuckoo," Sally said, twirling her forefinger near her temple. "I didn't know a thing about it until you just told me."

"Let's get back to the point," Joe said. "Why did you go back to the dining room the other day if it wasn't to draw a skull on Sonderstrom's napkin?"

Sally was clearly embarrassed. "Well—if you really want to know, I went back to change the place cards, so I'd be next to Sonderstrom at dinner. It was a sneaky thing to do, but—"

True or not, it was a reasonable explanation. Frank wasn't completely convinced, though. "If you're as innocent as you claim to be," he said, "why did you try to kill us just now?"

Sally's eyes widened. "Now I know you're wacko," she replied. "That's the craziest thing I've ever heard."

"Not so crazy," Joe said. "Somebody just shoved a block of stone off the upper level of the coliseum. It landed right where we were sitting. When Frank and I ran up the stairs, we found only one person up there. You. No one else could have pushed that stone over the edge, because no one else was there."

"You're serious, aren't you?" Sally demanded. "Well, I didn't drop any rock on you or anybody else, and that's that."

"Then who did?" Frank demanded.

Sally rolled her eyes in exasperation. "How should I know? Maybe somebody used a timer," she said in a sarcastic voice. "I'm not putting up with any more of this. Goodbye."

Before Frank and Joe could say another word, she spun on her heel and strode away.

"She sure seemed sincere," Joe said. "But maybe she's a good actress. I still think—"

"Wait a minute," Frank said urgently. "A timer— Joe, remember that I thought the floor was damp where the block had been?"

"Sure," Joe said. "What of it?"

"Suppose you took a block of stone and balanced it on one edge in such a way that it would tumble over when you let go," Frank continued. "But then suppose you propped it up with a block of ice. What would happen?"

Joe frowned. "When the ice melted, the block would fall over," he said. "And the spot where it had been would be damp."

"And you would have plenty of time to be far away by the time the block fell," Frank concluded. "You see what that means, don't you? The culprit was making sure he'd have an alibi for the attack. And since Sally didn't have an alibi, since she was still almost on the spot, that means she's the one person who almost certainly *didn't* do it. As for who did, I'm afraid it could have been anybody."

"Anybody who knew where to get a block of ice in the middle of the desert," Joe pointed out.

Frank nodded. "Good point. But we know where there's ice, don't we? In the coolers of cold drinks. Let's talk to Ahmed and find out if anybody took some."

When they reached the refreshment table, Ahmed was nowhere in sight. The other uniformed staff members were busy packing up the supplies for the trip back to the palace.

Joe went over to a tall, slim guy who was bending over to pick up one of the coolers. "Excuse me," he said. "Did you happen to see anybody take a big piece of ice a little while ago? It must have been about—"

The guy straightened up and whirled around to face Joe. With no warning, he threw the cooler straight at Joe and took off on a run.

Chapter

11

FRANK JUMPED FORWARD and helped his brother to his feet.

"I'm okay," Joe gasped. "Go after him!"

Frank set off at a run down the long, curving corridor in the direction that the waiter had taken.

Gail stepped in front of him. "Frank, wait. Please!" she cried. "You don't understand!"

Frank dodged around her and picked up the pace. The waiter wasn't in sight, but he couldn't be that far ahead. As he ran, Frank tried to envision the layout of the coliseum. As he recalled, this corridor was blocked off a little way farther on. There were only two sets of stairs still open that led to the upper levels, and he had already run past them. The exit, too, was behind them. Frank's quarry was apparently trapped.

Frank vaulted a fallen stone block. As he landed, he sensed movement to his left. An instant later, someone cannoned into him. Frank went flying sideways. He broke the fall with his shoulder and hip and lay still for a moment, stunned. When he pushed himself to his feet, he saw the flash of a white uniform jacket disappear around the curve of the corridor, heading back in the direction he had just come from.

"The exit," Frank muttered to himself as he sprinted after the fleeing man. "He must be trying to get to the exit." A few seconds later Frank had a clear view of a long stretch of the corridor, but the waiter was nowhere in sight.

Frank stopped and listened. There were shouts and the sound of pounding footsteps in the distance, but they weren't close enough to be the guy he was chasing. Where had he gone? Was he hiding in another niche, hoping to catch Frank off guard again? Frank began to walk quietly, looking carefully to each side. As he neared a gap in the wall, he thought he heard a faint sound. He edged up to the gap and peeked through. A shadowy, rubble-choked ramp led down toward the passages under the former arena.

Frank listened again, then clambered over the hip-high barrier and started down. At the bottom, he found himself in a long, narrow corridor. Most of its arched stone roof was intact. Here and there, stones had fallen from the ceiling, leaving jagged holes through which dust-filled beams of sunlight streamed in. There were low doorways in both directions along the length of the corridor. Frank checked out the first one. It led into a tiny, windowless room. What purpose had it served in Roman days? Could it have been a cell for prisoners? A cage for the wild animals that the gladiators would have to fight? If these stones could speak, their tales would be enough to chill anybody's blood.

Frank continued down the corridor, peering into each of the rooms. All were empty. He was nearing the end of the corridor when he heard the faint *swish* of a shoe brushing against stone. He spun around in time to see a man in white dashing in the direction of stairs leading back up to ground level.

Frank sprinted after him up the stairs and around the first corner. The waiter was a good runner but not in Frank's class. Frank narrowed the distance between them and was reaching out to grab him when the guy tripped on a loose stone and sprawled to the floor. Frank tumbled over him, skinning his palms on the rough paving stones. He scrambled to his knees and turned around.

The guy was already on his feet. Blood trickled from his nose and made a smear across his cheek. Desperate, he lowered his head and barreled blindly at Frank. Frank let him get close before dodging to the left and grabbing his arm. A moment later the man was lying helpless on his stomach with his arm twisted behind his back by Frank.

Frank was trying to catch his breath when he felt somebody kick his thigh. "Stop that, you bully," a voice shouted shrilly. "Can't you see you're hurting him? Let him go right now!"

Frank turned just as Gail stopped kicking him and began pounding on his back. "Hey, cut it out!" Frank said loudly.

At that point Joe came running up with a dozen or more people behind him. Joe immediately pulled Gail off Frank.

"Why don't you leave him alone? He didn't do anything to you!" she cried.

"Oh, no?" Joe replied. "What do you call slamming me in the stomach with a cooler—a sign of affection?"

Frank leaned close to his captive and said softly, "Okay, friend. I'm going to let you stand up now. But don't try anything. Agreed?"

"Sure," the guy gasped. "Whatever you say."

Frank released him, stood up, and took a step back. As the guy slowly pushed himself to his feet, Frank got a good look at him for the first time. He had jet black hair, olive skin, a prominent nose, and brows that jutted forward over soft eyes. Frank knew that he had seen him somewhere before, but where?

"Oh!" Gail gasped. "You're bleeding!"

The guy wiped his face on his sleeve, then reacted with surprise at the streak of blood.

Someone in the crowd passed him a handkerchief, which he pressed to his nose.

Gail turned on Frank and started to kick him in the shin. "You're horrible!" she cried.

As he backed out of reach, Frank stared at her, astonished and hurt. Why was she suddenly treating him like a monster after being so friendly for the last few days?

Suddenly he realized where he had seen the guy before—in the *souk* with his arm around Gail's shoulders. Whoever he was, Gail knew him very well.

"What's going on here?" a new voice demanded. It was Robert Delaplane, with Perry right behind him.

"Frank and Joe Hardy started chasing this poor guy for no reason at all," Gail declared. "And when they finally caught him, they started beating him up."

Stung by the injustice of this, Frank said, "He's a friend of yours, isn't he? I had a feeling that all these incidents were more than one person could handle. Have you two been working together the whole time?"

"Leave me alone!" Gail wailed.

"Now, see here, Frank," Perry said. "I don't know what you're getting at, but browbeating my daughter simply isn't the way to do it."

Perry's words stung. In that moment the Hardys' captive suddenly clasped his two hands together and swung them like a baseball bat right into Frank's stomach. Frank doubled over, and when he managed to straighten up again, the waiter was running in the direction of the exit. The crowd, confused by the rapid pace of events, let him pass. But Joe, close behind him, launched himself into a flying tackle. The guy crashed to the floor. Before he could recover, Joe dragged him up by the front of his shirt and slugged him.

"Daddy, stop him!" Gail cried. "He's going to kill him!"

Joe had his fist cocked ready for another blow, but at the sound of Gail's voice, he held it back.

Perry said, "I don't know who that fellow is or what this is all about, sweetheart, but he did just hit Frank when he wasn't looking. If I were Frank's brother, I'd probably have slugged him even harder than Joe did."

"Oh, it's hopeless," Gail sobbed, turning away. "Why won't anybody listen to me?"

"I'll listen," Frank said, touching her arm.

She shrugged him off and kept her back to him. Her shoulders were shaking.

"Look, all we did was go over to him and start to ask a couple of questions," Frank told her. "Suddenly he threw a drink cooler and started to run. Is that the way an innocent person acts? Of course we chased him. What would you expect us to do?"

"You kept hitting him," Gail said in a muffled voice. "He's all bloody."

"He banged his nose on the floor when he

tripped," Frank replied. Then, rubbing his stomach, he added, "And as far as hitting goes, I'd say we're pretty even. What I'd like to know is why you care so much what happens to him. He's not just one of the palace staff, is he? There's something between you two."

"Now hold on, Frank," Perry said, upset and confused. "Why don't you let me thrash this out with Gail in private?"

Before Frank could reply, Joe dragged the waiter over to them by his jacket collar. The waiter dabbed the handkerchief at his nose, then let his hand fall.

Perry stared at him, then slowly focused on Gail.

"It's okay, I know when I'm beat," the guy said. His accent was American with a hint of something else. "I won't try to get away again."

Delaplane had been watching from the circle of onlookers. Now he moved closer and tapped Joe on the shoulder. "Why are you holding this man?" he demanded. "What did he do?"

Frank said, "If our suspicions are correct, he's the one who—"

"Okay, I told you," the guy said roughly. "You caught me. Sure I did it."

Gail let out a gasp. "No, no, don't say anything!" she pleaded.

"Why not?" he replied. "I'm glad I did it. And if I had the chance, I'd do it again!"

Chapter

12

In the shocked silence that followed this confession, Perry Housman stepped forward. "I know you," he said. "At first I wasn't positive, but—you're Al Portago's boy, aren't you? Sure, that's it. Al's been bringing you to Explorers Guild dinners for several years now. A couple of years ago, in San Francisco, we all sat at the same table."

Joe exchanged glances with Frank. The waiter was the son of Portago, the gorilla expert whose career had been ruined by Thor Sonderstrom. That might clear up a lot of unanswered questions.

Gail put her arm around the guy's waist. "That's when Carlo and I first got to know each other," she said, giving Joe, Frank, and her father a defiant stare. "He was in boarding school in the States at the time. But we've been writing ever since he graduated and returned home."

Frank couldn't help feeling disappointed that Gail was involved with someone—not to mention the fact that it was someone who had just confessed to murder.

Perry shook his head. "I don't understand, son. What are you doing here in Tunisia working as a waiter? Didn't Gail tell me that you were enrolled in a university in France?"

"I was," Carlo replied. "But I took a leave of absence to help my father in his troubles."

Fred Estival asked, "How is he? A lot of us have been concerned about him."

Carlo gave Fred a hostile glance. "Don't talk to me," he said. "I know all about you. You were one of Sonderstrom's boys. You're one of the people who ruined my father. It's because of you that he left his life's work unfinished and retired, heartbroken."

"That's not fair," Fred protested to Carlo's back.

Joe decided it was time to take a hand. "It's no coincidence that you're working at the palace, is it?" he demanded. "You took the job because you knew Thor Sonderstrom was going to be here. You came to Tunisia to get revenge for what he did to your father."

"You bet I did," Carlo said. "A Tunisian friend at the university helped me get the papers

I needed to work here. I hope he doesn't get in trouble over this."

Alarmed, Perry stepped forward and said, "Hold on, Carlo. Maybe you'd better consult a lawyer before you say any more. This is very serious business, you know."

Before Carlo could respond, Frank said, "Your Tunisian friend isn't the only one you may get in trouble. You used Gail in your plot against Sonderstrom, too, didn't you?"

"Frank!" Perry exclaimed.

Carlo acted indignant. Putting his arm around Gail's shoulders, he said, "I did not! She tried to talk me out of it, as a matter of fact. But when she realized that I was determined to go ahead, she promised she wouldn't tell anyone who I was. And she didn't. She's wonderful!"

"So you did the whole thing yourself," Joe said. "You drew that skull on Sonderstrom's napkin, stole Ahmed's scorpion, and slipped it under Sonderstrom's hat at breakfast—"

"I'm going to pay Ahmed for his scorpion," Carlo said, breaking in. "I would have done it right away, but I was worried he might mention it to someone."

"One thing I don't understand," Frank said. "How did you manage to make sure that Sonderstrom, and only Sonderstrom, got the poisoned mushrooms?"

Carlo gave him a puzzled frown. "Poisoned mushrooms? What poisoned mushrooms? I don't—"

His jaw dropped as his face turned pale. "You think I *poisoned* him? He died by accident—an allergic reaction or something. The police said so."

"But yesterday they didn't know that a deadly enemy of Sonderstrom was working in the kitchen," Frank pointed out. "When they find out, they may decide to reassess the cause of death."

"Frank, don't be ridiculous!" Gail burst out. "Carlo didn't kill anybody. All he did was play a couple of practical jokes. And believe me, Sonderstrom deserved it after what he did to his dad."

"Listen, I'm not going to pretend I was sorry when I found out that Sonderstrom was dead," Carlo said earnestly. "But I didn't kill him. As a matter of fact, I had a couple more surprises planned for him. Too bad I didn't get a chance to carry them out."

"Listen," Perry said, glancing around at the circle of fascinated onlookers. "Why don't we continue this discussion in private."

Frank and Joe stepped aside to allow Carlo and Gail to pass. Then they followed the couple down the corridor, through one of the passages that led to the interior of the arena. A few people tried to go with them, but Perry barred the way.

When they reached a cell about halfway around

the arena, Gail and Carlo pulled themselves up onto a low stone wall.

Leaning in the scant shade of an archway beside them, Joe asked, "What were your duties at the banquet last night?"

Carlo seemed a little dazed as he said, "Let's see—I helped set up the buffet, laying out the cold dishes and getting the heating units ready for the warm ones. Once the doors opened, I was supposed to carry out the refills. But I traded jobs with another guy and stayed in the kitchen getting the refill platters ready. I was nervous that someone in the guild might recognize me."

"Then you weren't in the dining room at all while the guests were serving themselves?" Frank asked.

Carlo shook his head. "No. And I never went near those mushrooms. Ask the others in the kitchen if you don't believe me. Or ask the fellow who prepared them. He wouldn't *let* anybody near them. He must have been worried that somebody would be poisoned."

"Somebody was," Joe said grimly. After a brief pause, he continued, "A few minutes ago, a block of stone fell from the top level of the coliseum. It nearly killed my brother and me. And when I tried to ask you about it, you threw a cooler at me and ran away. That's not the way an innocent person acts."

Carlo gave him a sullen look. "I knew you guys

were trying to find out who'd pulled those stunts against Sonderstrom."

His glance at Gail made it clear how he had kept track of what the Hardys were doing.

"I was afraid you'd figured out who I was," he went on. "I panicked. I didn't even think, I just threw the chest and took off."

"He was scared, can't you understand that?" Gail demanded. "It hasn't been easy for him."

Frank let her comment fly by. "But before that, you'd rigged the stone to fall on us, hadn't you?" he said. "That was pretty clever, the way you did it."

"I tell you, I didn't do it," Carlo said angrily. "I can even prove it. Ask any of the other people working at the refreshment table. Ask Ahmed. I was grilling hamburgers the whole time, from the moment the charcoal was ready until you came over to question me. I volunteered for the job, because that way I could keep my back to all the people lining up for lunch."

"You've got to believe him," Gail added. "If Carlo says he didn't do it, he didn't."

"Look," Carlo said with a hint of desperation in his voice. "If I don't get back to work, I'm going to be fired. Don't worry, I'm not planning to run away. Now that you know who I am, what would be the point?"

Joe studied Carlo's face, then turned his back to him. "What do you think?" he asked Frank in an undertone.

"We don't have enough evidence to have him arrested," Frank murmured in reply. "Not that the cops seem that interested in the case anyway."

Joe nodded his agreement. Aloud, he said, "Okay, Carlo. But we're going to check your story very carefully."

"Go ahead," Carlo retorted. "I'm not worried. I told you the truth." He gave Gail a hug, then edged past Perry and walked quickly back toward the refreshment area.

Perry said, "I hope you boys are satisfied. I'm as surprised as anyone to find Carlo here, but I can assure you that he's a fine young man."

Gail started to walk away. Frank stepped in front of her.

"How about you, Gail?" he asked. "Did you climb up to the top level of the coliseum?"

Her cheeks turned pink. "You know very well I didn't," she said. "Remember? You asked me and my dad if we wanted to go with you, and we decided not to."

Frank persisted. "But what about later on? Say, a little before that stone fell?"

The color in Gail's face deepened. "Are you always so suspicious of everybody?" she demanded. "I'm surprised you have any friends left."

Frank flinched. Was this the same girl he had thought was so cute and friendly only hours before?

"Hey, hold on," Joe interjected. "That's not fair. Your boyfriend's the one who's been sneaking around, playing dirty tricks on people."

"On *one* person," Gail retorted, "who deserved it. And I thought it was a terrible idea. I tried to talk him out of it. But I couldn't. Carlo says his dad is a changed man—he wanders around their house outside Rome like a robot, and Carlo can't bear it. He felt he had to do something. And then, to see the way everybody at the conference was crowding around Sonderstrom, acting as if he were some kind of great man just because they wanted money from his foundation. It made Carlo even madder."

"You still haven't answered me," Frank reminded her. "Did you go to the top level?"

"I don't have to tell you," Gail said hotly. "But just to give you a cheap thrill, I will. Sure I did. I used my folding helicopter to fly up there, threw a rock at you, and then came back down, eating a tuna fish sandwich the whole time. Are you happy now, Mr. Nosy?"

She didn't wait for a reply. Sidestepping Frank, she strode away.

"I hope she calms down," Joe said.

"So do I," Frank replied somberly. "Let's go check on Carlo's whereabouts today."

After talking to Ahmed and three other members of the staff, Frank said, "Okay. So Carlo has an ironclad alibi for the whole time we've been here *and* for last night's banquet. But Gail doesn't. And we know she's been helping him. He could easily have slipped her the block of ice and told her what to do with it."

"Do you really think Gail would try to kill us?" Joe demanded.

"It's hard to believe," Frank said finally. "But what if she just wanted to scare us and her aim was better than she meant it to be?"

"She wouldn't have any good reason to do that unless she and Carlo were guilty of something worse than a couple of pranks," Joe pointed out.

"I know—that occurred to me," Frank said. "We have to face it. Carlo *was* in the kitchen the whole time during the banquet, just as he said. But what if he filched one of the mushrooms earlier, while it was still deadly, then slipped it to Gail to put on Sonderstrom's plate?"

Joe shook his head. "I don't believe she'd try to kill Sonderstrom any more than she'd try to kill us. But how about this? Let's say Carlo told her that the mushroom would just make him sick? Who knows, maybe he believed it, too. Then when Sonderstrom dropped dead, there they were, accomplices in a murder without meaning to be."

"Could be," Frank said, nodding. "What we have to do when we get back to the palace is double-check Carlo's story, then try to trace Gail's movements during the banquet."

"Right," Joe said. "Not to mention staying out of the way of falling stones."

On their way to board the bus for the ride back, Frank and Joe saw Gail and Carlo holding hands and talking earnestly. She noticed them and pointedly turned away. The Hardys took seats near the rear of the bus. A few moments later Perry came down the aisle and stopped next to them. His face was set in an unfriendly expression.

"I have to congratulate you fellows," he said. "You told me you were going to find out who played those jokes on Thor, and you did it. Now we can all relax and enjoy the rest of the conference, right?"

"Not quite," Frank said. "Sonderstrom's still dead. And it's only because we moved fast that Joe and I aren't dead, too. There's a killer loose, and we intend to find out who it is before he or she strikes again."

A muscle in Perry's jaw tensed, and the vein in his temple stood out. "Thor's death was a terrible accident," he said. "I spoke to Commissaire Meddour this morning before we left, and he's still convinced of that. As for what happened today, that coliseum is two thousand years old. You've got to expect pieces of it to fall off. It was just bad luck that you were sitting under one of them when it fell."

Frank was about to tell Perry about the scratches

that proved someone had dragged the stone block to the edge, but before he could, Perry leaned over, jabbed his forefinger into Frank's chest, and said, "I'm just going to say this one more time—quit snooping. I'd hate to see anything happen to you. Meddling in matters that are none of your business can be dangerous."

Chapter

13

PERRY GLARED silently at the Hardys for a long moment, then went back to his seat. Frank and Joe were shocked. This man had been a hero of theirs. Recently he had become a friend as well. They wouldn't be in Tunisia if it weren't for him, but now he was sounding like anything but a friend. Hadn't he just ordered them to drop their investigation and told them that they'd be sorry if they didn't?

"There's only one explanation for the way he's acting," Frank said. "He must think that Gail is mixed up with Carlo's activities and that Carlo is behind Sonderstrom's death."

"Would he really suspect his own daughter of being an accomplice to murder?" Joe wondered.

"He might. After all, we do, more or less,"

Frank pointed out. "But even if he's convinced that she's innocent, he might be afraid that she'll *look* guilty. Since the police are satisfied, why not just shove the whole business under the rug? On the other hand, Perry may really think that Sonderstrom's death was an accident and that we're just imagining things."

"If he does," Joe muttered, "I know a terrific bridge in Brooklyn that I'd be happy to sell him cheap."

An hour later the bus pulled up at the palace. As Frank and Joe were starting up the steps to the entrance, they noticed a tall man in horn-rimmed glasses.

"Isn't he the guy who fixed those mushrooms?" Joe said to Frank. "What was his name, Ferber? We ought to have a talk with him."

They went over and introduced themselves.

"Oh, sure, the detectives," he replied. "I hear that you think Thor Sonderstrom was murdered."

"We don't yet have any proof," Frank said cautiously. "But we certainly think that the way he died calls for more investigation."

To Frank's astonishment, Ferber said, "I tend to agree. The police theory, that he died of an allergic reaction, seems unlikely to me. I don't suppose the police doctors in Tunisia run into it very often, but to my mind, his symptoms seemed much more like those of a person exposed to a powerful nerve toxin."

"But isn't that just what those mushrooms of yours contain?" Joe asked.

Ferber rolled his eyes and gave a loud sigh. "I'm beginning to wish I had never heard of the Explorers Guild banquet," he said. "Let me explain one more time. Raw, those mushrooms do contain an organic compound that's quite poisonous. But it also happens to be very sensitive to even moderate heat. At anything over fifty-five degrees Celsius, it breaks down and becomes totally harmless."

"Are you sure of that?" Frank asked.

"Perfectly sure," he replied impatiently. "These mushrooms are found only on a small island in Indonesia. The native people of the island cook and eat them regularly. Once cooked, they're harmless. Would I have risked serving them otherwise?"

Joe asked, "How do you know all this, Mr. Ferber?"

"Please call me Paul," he replied. "And I know it because that's my job. I'm an ethnopharmacologist. I travel around the world, studying the diets and medical treatments of other cultures. It may be that our next 'miracle drug' won't be the product of some high-tech laboratory, but that we'll owe it to the knowledge and traditions of some small tribe in Amazonia or the hills of Nepal."

"That sounds like really exciting and useful work," Frank said. "I'd love to hear more about it. But right now, I'm still wondering about those mushrooms. You say that as soon as they're cooked, they're harmless. But what if a few of them *didn't* get cooked but were deliberately slipped in with the cooked ones?"

Ferber shook his head. "I haven't been able to sleep, thinking of all the possibilities. That is a possibility, of course. So this morning I returned to the kitchen and did an experiment. I didn't have any more of mine, but I cooked some ordinary mushrooms in exactly the same manner. Then I put them in a serving dish and measured their internal temperature. It was nearly seventy degrees Celsius—about one hundred sixty degrees Fahrenheit. And as I said, the toxin in my mushrooms breaks down at around fifty-five degrees Celsius. If someone did put some raw mushrooms into the dish of cooked ones, the heat would be enough to render the toxin harmless within a minute or two."

"And if the dish cooled off?" Joe suggested.

"No good," Frank said. "Remember? The hot dishes were kept on electric plate warmers to keep them from cooling off."

Frank turned to Ferber. "If I understand you," he said, "you're telling us that there is no way Sonderstrom could have been poisoned by the mushrooms in that dish, even if someone got hold of some raw ones, slipped them into the serving dish, and arranged for Sonderstrom to get them."

"That's correct," Ferber said.

"In that case Sonderstrom's death must have

been a freak accident just as the police think," Frank said, almost disappointed. "We've been wasting our time."

"No, wait," Joe said. "How about this? Sonderstrom takes a couple of spoonfuls of the cooked mushrooms and puts them on his plate. What happens? They immediately start cooling off, right? Then before he starts eating them, somebody slips some raw ones in with them. By that time, the cooked ones have cooled off so much that the poison ones remain poison."

"I think Sonderstrom would have noticed," Ferber said. "You see, these mushrooms have another peculiarity. Raw, they're pale yellow, almost white. It's only when you cook them that they turn that bright reddish color. If you mixed the raw with the cooked, the difference would be instantly apparent. Do you begin to see why I'm so certain that my mushrooms had nothing to do with Sonderstrom's death?"

Frank tried to keep his frustration from showing as he asked, "Then what *do* you think killed him?"

Ferber pulled a white handkerchief from his hip pocket, removed his glasses, and carefully polished them. "Well, I'm no detective," he said, "but I do like to read mysteries. And it occurs to me that if I were planning to poison someone, I couldn't think of a better place to do it than the Explorers Guild banquet. With all those odd dishes, the chances would be excellent that the investigators would end up blaming the victim's death on one of them and not look any farther."

"Which is just what's happening," Frank said. "But that would mean that the murderer came here prepared to kill Sonderstrom. So whatever his motive might be, it couldn't be something that developed in the last day or two."

"I suppose that's true. I hadn't really thought it through," Ferber said. He glanced at his watch and added, "But you'll have to excuse me. There's someone here who lived among the Inuit of Greenland and is going to tell me about their medical lore."

Ferber left Frank and Joe standing alone on the broad steps of the palace. "Let's take a walk," Frank suggested. "I don't feel like dealing with anyone just now."

They passed through the gardens to the beach. As they walked along the surf, Frank said, "If Ferber's idea is right, Sally and Doug are pretty low on our list of suspects. We're assuming that their motive was to keep Sonderstrom from going back on his board's approval of their grants. But they had no way of knowing what had happened with their grants until after they got here. Remember, Fred said the list of approved grants was closely guarded. So they had no reason to come prepared to murder Sonderstrom."

"It's looking pretty bleak for Carlo, isn't it," Joe said. "He admitted that he came here solely to take revenge on Sonderstrom."

"But according to him and the other waiters, he wasn't in the dining room at all during the banquet," Frank reminded Joe. "Of course, Carlo's buddies could be covering for him. But if he really *wasn't* there, how could he have administered the poison? On the other hand, Fred Estival also came here furious at Sonderstrom. And he was just a couple of people ahead of us in the serving line. I don't know how he could have slipped poison to Sonderstrom without anybody's noticing, but at least he was in the same room with the victim."

Joe picked up a pebble and flung it at the surf. "I'm beginning to wonder if Perry isn't right," he said. "Maybe Sonderstrom did die from an allergic reaction, and it's just a coincidence that so many people have reasons to have wanted him dead."

Frank shook his head. "If Perry is still speaking to us, we should ask him if he's found out what's in the police lab report. And Fred's still a suspect, too, *if* we can figure out how he could have poisoned Sonderstrom."

Joe took a deep breath. "Okay, let's get to work."

After the presentation, the conference participants strolled along the seafront boulevard to a brooding stone fortress just past the *souk* called the Ribat. Frank and Joe noticed Fred in the crowd and joined him. He seemed more relaxed now, as if Sonderstrom's death had allowed him to put his anger and resentment aside.

"This place might look familiar to you," Fred remarked as they walked into the shadow of the fort's high, sheer stone walls. "It's been used in lots of movies, as everything from a biblical walled city to a medieval castle."

A winding ramp led up to a single narrow entrance a dozen feet above ground level. They walked through a shadowy tunnel and found themselves in a courtyard surrounded by twenty-foot-high walls. A set of rough stone steps with no railings was set into one of the walls, leading to the next level, from which the Hardys could hear a buzz of conversation.

"What was this place?" Joe asked, gazing around curiously.

"A combination monastery and fort," Fred told him. "The oldest section dates all the way back to the eighth century, after the Arab conquest of North Africa. They built fortresses like this all along the coast to protect their new possessions against European raiders. From the top of the watchtower, they could spot any approaching ships and give the alarm."

"I'd like to see what the view is like from the top," Frank said, leaning back to look at the tall, slender tower of stone. "Can we go up?"

"If you don't mind the climb," Fred replied. "It's over seventy feet high—as tall as a seven-story building."

At the base of the tower, they found people lining up to duck through the low arched doorway and climb the watchtower. Sally and Doug turned and said hello, but Gail and Perry, just ahead of them, pretended not to notice the Hardys. Frank shrugged at Joe. If they wanted to stay mad, let them.

Inside, narrow, irregular stone steps wound upward in the dark. Frank's shoulders brushed the central pillar on one side and the rough tower wall on the other. Every so often, a tiny slit in the wall gave him a glimpse of the city or the sea far below.

The top platform was no more than six feet across and already crowded. Gail and Perry made their way to the edge, next to Delaplane, who was scanning the coastline with a pair of binoculars. Frank found himself hemmed in and saw with a touch of envy that Joe had managed to reach the knee-high parapet with its stunning views.

As more people arrived at the head of the stairs, the crowd shifted. All at once Frank heard an alarmed shout. He spun around and saw with horror that Joe was falling sideways and would be over the parapet in an instant. Frank's heart sank as he realized that he couldn't possibly reach his brother in time to save him.

Chapter

14

AS JOE FELT himself start to fall, he flung his arms wide and twisted at the waist, trying to heave himself back onto the tiny platform. He was too far off balance, though, and began to topple over the low stone parapet. He was staring down at the pavement far below.

Around him, people had been shouting, and suddenly hands gripped his arms. For a second he hung in space, but then he could feel himself being pulled back to safety. When he made it over the parapet, Joe straightened, took a deep breath, and looked around. Perry was holding his left arm, and Gail, his right. Joe tried to speak, but the inside of his mouth felt as if it were stuffed with cotton. He had to swallow before he could say, "Thanks. That was close."

"You should be more careful," Perry said, obviously concerned. "What happened, did you get dizzy?"

"Are you okay?" asked Gail, white faced.

"I'm fine, thanks to you two," Joe said.

Frank was pushing through the crowd to his side. Joe met his worried glance and said, "I'm okay. But I'd just as soon go back to ground level—by way of the stairs, if possible."

Joe was glad to let Frank lead the way down the steep, winding staircase. His knees still felt shaky. Once they reached the courtyard, he glanced around to be sure they weren't overheard, then said, "Frank, somebody pushed me up there."

Frank stared at him. "Are you sure?"

"I can't be sure that it was deliberate," Joe replied. "The crowd was pretty thick, but somebody certainly elbowed me in the back hard. If Perry and Gail hadn't grabbed me in time, I would have gone over the edge." He looked up at the watchtower and shuddered.

"Any idea who did it?" Frank demanded.

"I was admiring the view," Joe replied, "and not paying attention to the people standing in back of me. Gail and Perry were closest, I guess. But the platform is so small that almost anybody could have given me a shove."

"If it hadn't been for Perry and Gail, you'd be a goner," Frank said.

"I know that," Joe said somberly. "And I hate

to think that either of them would have tried to kill me. But maybe they meant to give me a scare. What if Gail pushed me, knowing that she was near enough to stop me from actually falling?"

Frank was unconvinced. "What if she had missed?"

"Fred was up there, too," Joe added.

"All our suspects were except for Carlo," Frank pointed out. "So that's no real help. But there is one thing—now we know for sure that Sonderstrom was murdered."

Joe was puzzled. "We do?"

"Yes. Our investigation must be a big threat to somebody," Frank explained. "Why else make two different attempts on our lives in one day— first at the coliseum, then now? Who are we threatening so much? We already know who was harassing Sonderstrom—Carlo, he's already confessed. The only other mystery we're trying to solve is who may have murdered Sonderstrom. And that can't threaten anybody unless Sonderstrom really was murdered."

"I see your point," Joe said. "I just wish I had as much confidence in our investigation as the murderer seems to. As far as I can see, we're pretty much at a dead end."

Frank was silent for a few moments. At last he said, "What do you do when you find yourself at a dead end? You back up and try another road. We've spent practically all our time concentrating on how the murder was carried out. But a murder involves two people, the murderer and the victim. It's time we concentrated on the victim."

"We know what Sonderstrom was like," Joe protested. "We watched him in action. Everybody disliked him."

"Okay, but only a nut kills somebody because he doesn't *like* him," Frank replied. "And Sonderstrom was probably disliked his whole life. What made somebody kill him now?"

Joe shrugged. "If you keep pouring water into a glass, sooner or later it overflows. It just happened to overflow here, yesterday. Why? What do you have in mind?"

"I'm just remembering the way Sonderstrom's mood changed in the middle of the afternoon," Frank replied. "Remember when he came out on his balcony, whistling? Fred said Sonderstrom had just decided to give somebody a really hard time."

Joe thought for a moment. "He could have found out that Carlo was responsible for those dirty tricks," he suggested.

"I don't see how," Frank said. "And if he had, he would have gotten Carlo fired right away. No, I think something must have happened. But how can we find out what?"

Joe snapped his fingers. "Sally!" he exclaimed. "Remember the way she was hanging on him yesterday? If anything changed his mood, she would have noticed for sure."

"Let's find out," Frank replied.

They found Sally with Doug in the small museum on the ground floor of the fortress, holding hands and gazing at each other instead of the exhibits. When Frank said that they had some questions about Sonderstrom, Sally followed them out to the courtyard.

"Sonderstrom's state of mind yesterday afternoon?" she repeated after Frank explained what they wanted. "I guess I'd say watchful. All the time I was talking to him, he kept looking at people as if he was wondering about them."

"Did you notice his mood change?" Joe asked.

Sally tugged thoughtfully at her earlobe. "Well, yes, now that you mention it," she said. "We were talking about the session on Gypsies when Ahmed brought him a letter in what looked to me like an express-delivery envelope. He glanced through it, then suddenly took off."

Frank asked urgently, "Do you have any idea who the letter was from? Or what it was about?"

Sally shook her head.

"And Sonderstrom didn't say anything at all?" Joe insisted.

She frowned. "No, not a word."

Joe and Frank looked at each other. "Ahmed!" they said in unison.

"Let's head for the palace," Joe added. "Thanks, Sally."

They found the boy in his family's modest apartment at the back of the palace. When they

138

asked him about the incident, he said, "Oh, yes, I remember very well. The letter is very important, so I go at once to give it to Mr. Sonderstrom."

Frank asked, "Did you happen to notice who sent it?"

"No, but you bet I notice the stamp," Ahmed said with a big grin. "It is from a country I never hear of before. Do you want to see?"

Joe's jaw dropped. "You have the letter?"

"No, no, only the envelope," Ahmed replied. "It's right here."

He rummaged through a cardboard carton and produced a large multicolored envelope covered with lettering in a foreign alphabet.

Joe took it and studied the return address. "It's from a Professor Ulyanov at a university in Alma Ata, in Kazakhstan," he reported.

"That's one of the former Soviet republics," Frank said. "Near Mongolia. What do you suppose he had to say to Sonderstrom that was so urgent?"

Joe said, "Let's call him and find out."

It took over half an hour to find English-speaking operators in Tunisia and Kazakhstan who could help put the call through. Also, there was a good deal of static on the line. But finally Frank reached the professor, who spoke English. Joe hovered nearby, trying to imagine the meaning of Frank's *uh-huh*s and *really*s. At last, his brother hung up.

"Well?" Joe demanded.

Frank gave him an odd look. "You know that lost culture in Central Asia that Delaplane wrote a prize-winning book about?"

"Sure," Joe replied. *"Passage in Time.* Fascinating stuff. What about it?"

Frank shook his head in amazement. "Well, get this. According to Professor Ulyanov, the culture doesn't exist. At all. Delaplane made up the whole thing. When Sonderstrom read that letter yesterday afternoon, he learned the truth about Delaplane's fraud. But before he could tell the world about it, he died."

As JOE STARED at him in disbelief, Frank continued. "If the truth comes out, Delaplane's reputation will be ruined. He'll lose his university position. They might even take back his Pulitzer. He'll be ruined for life."

"Now there's a motive for murder," Joe said. "But you can't tell me that Delaplane brought a little bottle of poison with him to Tunisia just in case he needed to kill someone. And even if he did, we've still got to figure out how he gave the poison to Sonderstrom."

"You know," Frank said slowly, "if I'd just found out that Sonderstrom was a terrible threat to me and decided that I had to eliminate him, the first thing I'd think of is those mushrooms."

"Which weren't poisonous once they were

cooked," Joe said. "We've been through all that."

"Yes—but suppose Delaplane managed to get hold of a raw one?" Frank replied. "He could have extracted the poison and then given it to Sonderstrom. And even if it showed up in an autopsy, everyone would simply assume that Thor had eaten a mushroom that wasn't thoroughly cooked. Does that make sense?"

Joe stared at him open-mouthed. "Frank!" he said. "I bet we saw him do it! Remember when, right before the banquet, we were talking to Sonderstrom, and Delaplane came over with two drinks? He handed one to Sonderstrom. He must have put the mushroom juice in Sonderstrom's drink!"

"It's possible," Frank said. "But however well it all hangs together, it's still just guesswork. What we need are answers from Delaplane. Let's go find him."

They hurried back to the Ribat. The first person they saw was Perry Housman. Frank felt a little ashamed for having suspected the former astronaut of trying to cover up a crime. He went over and asked, "Is Robert Delaplane around?"

Perry scratched his head. "He ought to be," he replied. "But I haven't seen him in the last half hour or so. As a matter of fact, I have a message for him."

"Oh?" Frank said, keeping his voice casual. "Would you like us to pass it on if we see him?"

"Sure, if you wouldn't mind," Perry said. "He should call Philippe, at Aero Monde, right away. Here's the number."

"I'll tell him," Frank promised, taking the slip of paper. As Perry walked away, he turned to Joe and said, "Do you want to call this Philippe guy or start searching for Delaplane?"

"I'll make the call," Joe replied. "I saw a pay phone on our way here. Good hunting."

Most of the guests were on the second level, watching a man in native costume dancing with a tall pottery jar on his head. Frank carefully scanned the crowd, but Delaplane wasn't there. He wasn't on the next level either. Had he already left the Ribat?

As Frank returned to the main courtyard, Joe dashed up. "Listen," he said breathlessly. "Philippe is a pilot with his own air charter company. Delaplane hired him for a flight to Rome this evening. The reason Philippe called was to tell him that they'll have to leave earlier than planned if Delaplane expects to connect with the scheduled flight from Rome to Moscow."

"Moscow!" Frank repeated. "I can guess his next stop after that—Alma Ata. He must be planning to silence Professor Ulyanov, too. We've got to stop him, but where is he?"

"Oh, Frank, Joe," Perry called, striding across the courtyard. "There you are. Don't worry about that message for Bob Delaplane. I gave it to him a couple of minutes ago. Poor guy—he can't even stay long enough to be inaugurated as president of the Explorers Guild."

"What?" Joe exclaimed. "Where's he going?"

"To Russia," Perry replied. "Apparently one of the people who worked closely with him is very ill. The doctors don't give him long to live. Bob is leaving tonight to be by his side. I have to say I admire him for that."

Frank asked urgently, "Did you say you saw him a couple of minutes ago? Where? I have to speak to him before he goes."

"He was about to leave," Perry said. "He was going by the palace to pick up his bag, then taking a cab to the airport."

"We may still be able to catch him," Frank told Joe. "Let's go."

They dashed out of the fortress and onto the wide boulevard that led along the beach to the palace. On the right was the sea, and on the left, the wall surrounding the *souk*. The sun was already setting, but there was still enough light to see. There were no cars on the road, and only one pedestrian, about two hundred yards ahead. It had to be Delaplane. Frank and Joe began to run after him, taking long strides that ate up the distance. They had cut the gap in half when he apparently heard them coming. After a hurried glance over his shoulder, he ran across the road and through the gateway to the *souk*.

"Oh, no!" Joe cried, panting, as they angled across the road to the gate. "We'll never find him in that maze!"

"He doesn't know his way either," Frank replied. "And he's running out of time."

They sprinted through the archway and paused to orient themselves. It was very different from their last visit. Metal shutters covered the fronts of the shops, and the narrow, curving lanes were practically empty. From an open second-floor window, a bearded man in a white skullcap peered down at Frank and Joe, then turned to look at something farther along the lane. On a hunch, Frank said, "That way."

They walked quickly around the curve. Just then, a shadowy figure darted into a narrow alley. Joe, the sprinter of the Hardy family, was instantly on his trail. Frank loped after them.

The alley was barely wider than a hallway, with pitch-black stretches where the roofs of the ramshackle houses met overhead. Frank slipped on what felt like a melon rind and almost fell. After that he moved more cautiously.

Joe suddenly surged out of the darkness. "Did you see him?" he demanded.

"No," Frank replied.

"This passage comes to a dead end in a courtyard," Joe continued. "He isn't there. He must have slipped into a side passage and hidden until we went by. We'll never find him now."

"Yes, we will," Frank replied. "He has to leave

the *souk* to take that plane. If he hasn't already escaped, we'll catch him at the entrance."

They were turning to go back, when Frank heard a faint noise like a shoe scraping on stone. It had come from a dark, covered passage. Frank touched Joe's shoulder and pointed, then started to feel his way along the narrow passage. After a dozen feet, it branched out. He paused to listen. A faint sound came from the right. He followed it and found himself in a large, irregularly shaped courtyard with half a dozen doorways in the surrounding walls. There was no one in sight.

Frank peered over his shoulder at Joe, who was as puzzled as he was. At that moment there was a rumbling sound from one of the darkest corners of the court. Frank turned to see a large wooden barrel rolling toward him. He jumped aside, but his shoe caught on a paving stone and he fell. A searing pain shot up his leg as the barrel rolled over his foot and ankle. He let out a gasp.

"Frank! Are you all right?" Joe demanded, rushing forward and bending over him.

As Frank pushed himself up from the pavement, a shadowy form darted behind Joe's back and vanished into the passage that led to the street. "Delaplane!" Frank blurted. "He's escaping!"

Without a word, Joe spun around and dashed after the killer. Frank staggered to his feet and limped after them, trying to ignore the pain in his ankle. He reached the lane in time to see

Joe launch himself in a flying tackle that brought Delaplane to the ground.

"Okay, okay, I know when I'm beat," Delaplane choked out. He sat up and brushed a scraped place on his chin with the back of his hand. "I was never much of a runner."

Joe took his arm and dragged him to his feet. "Come on," he said. "We've got a phone call to make to Commissaire Meddour. And you can cancel that flight to Moscow, too. You're going to be spending a long time in Tunisia—in jail."

"Bob, how could you?" Perry demanded. He and the Hardys were in Perry's room at the palace, keeping an eye on the killer while they waited for Meddour to arrive.

"Thor would have ruined me," Delaplane muttered. "And so many people here had reasons to hate him, it seemed like the perfect place to get rid of him."

Frank said, "We worked out that you must have poisoned his drink. But why on earth did he accept a drink from your hands when he knew what a terrible threat he was to you?"

Delaplane sniffed. "He didn't know that I knew. The boy who took him that letter from Ulyanov asked me if I knew where Thor was. The moment I saw that it was from Kazakhstan, I knew what was in it. Ulyanov had already threatened to expose me. So I filched three or four of Ferber's mushrooms, extracted their juice, and waited for my chance. After Thor was dead, I went to his room and retrieved Ulyanov's letter. But I couldn't find the envelope. That was my mistake."

"One of them," Perry said grimly. "And to think that I nearly caught you in Thor's room."

"You were the one who rigged that block of stone to fall on us today?" Joe asked. "And tried to push me off the tower of the Ribat?"

"I didn't have any choice," Delaplane said again. "The police were satisfied. But you wouldn't leave well enough alone. You kept poking around. I had to scare you off somehow."

"And instead," Frank said as Meddour came through the doorway followed by two uniformed officers, "all you accomplished was to convince us that we were on the right track."

"Is he crazy?" Gail demanded. She and her father were sitting with Frank, Joe, and half a dozen others on the terrace overlooking the beach. Commissaire Meddour had just left with Robert Delaplane in his custody.

"You'll have to ask a psychiatrist that," Joe replied. "Crazy or not, he almost managed to get away with murder."

Paul Ferber said, "I am furious at myself. I was so pleased when he showed an interest in my work. I told him all about those mushrooms, and when he asked, of course I showed them to him."

"You couldn't have guessed that he was planning to steal some," Frank said.

"No, of course not. But it was irresponsible to let anybody have access to something I knew was poisonous," Ferber replied.

"Don't be too hard on yourself," Doug said. "He could have managed without you. Poison is not that hard to come by."

Frank looked up. Carlo had just come out on the terrace, still in his staff uniform. He walked over and sat down next to Gail, who took his hand. Frank brushed aside the tiny feeling of disappointment and asked Carlo, "Will you be going back to school now?"

Carlo shook his head. "No. I called my father in Italy just now and told him that if he would take up his research again, I would help him. We're off to Central Africa as soon as we can find financial support."

"Africa? Oh, Carlo," Gail said in a voice full of emotion. Then she managed a smile and added, "That's wonderful for you *and* your dad!"

Fred Estival joined them, seeming dazed.

"Is something wrong?" Frank asked him.

Fred blinked a couple of times, then brushed a lock of hair back from his forehead. "Wrong?" he said. "No, not at all. Just the opposite. I got a phone call just now from Fin Rorik, the chair of the Eriksson Foundation board. They want me back as executive director."

"Great!" Gail shouted. Hans came over to clap Fred on the back.

Fred grinned shyly. "I said yes, of course," he

continued. "Then I told him that my first official act would be to confirm the decisions made at the most recent board meeting and communicate them to the grant recipients as soon as possible."

He paused and spoke to Sally and Doug. "Congratulations. We're expecting great things from both of you."

Perry Housman stood up and shook hands with Fred and Doug, then gave Sally a kiss on the cheek. When the cheers and applause died down, he looked around with a twinkle in his eye.

"We'd better get some sleep," he said. "We have an important membership meeting of the Explorers Guild tomorrow morning, you know. We need to choose a new president. And the first item on the agenda after that will be to vote honorary life memberships in the guild to Frank and Joe Hardy."

More cheers and applause followed.

"Thanks, Perry," Frank said, getting to his feet. "It'll be a real honor to belong to an organization with members like you."

"It sure will," Joe said, standing up next to Frank. "But does that mean we have to come to the annual banquet every year?"

"Don't worry, Joe," Perry said. "As a special favor to you, we'll be sure to serve pizza—*without* mushrooms!"

Frank and Joe's next case:

The Hardys have come to the West Coast for Christmas break, and they're about to tackle a case of pro football foul play. Following the suspicious death of their star player, the San Diego Sharks have hit the skids, and the owner is convinced it's a setup. The boys agree to go undercover and are soon mixing it up with some hard and heavy hitters. Talk of contraband in the locker room, of blackmail and bribery, lead Frank and Joe to believe that a crime syndicate has infiltrated the team. Big money is at stake, and there's no telling how far the syndicate will go to protect its interests. The blitz is on, and if the Hardys don't come up with a few trick plays of their own, they could face sudden death ... in *Illegal Procedure,* Case #95 in The Hardy Boys Casefiles™.

THE HARDY BOYS CASEFILES™